GRIMM

THE ILLUSTRATED

FAIRY TALES

OF THE BROTHERS GRIMM

by

Jacob & Wilhelm Grimm

Content

Hansel & Grethel   6

Little Red-Cap   18

The Frog-King   24

King Thrushbeard   32

The Bremen Town-Musicians   40

Hans in Luck   46

Snow-White & Rose-Red   54

The Star-Money   64

Mother Holle   66

The Wolf and the Seven Little Kids   72

The Valiant Little Tailor   78

The Wishing-Table, Gold-Ass, and the Cudgel in the Sack   92

Thumbling   108

Jorinda & Joringel   118

Rapunzel   124

Briar-Rose   132

Rumpelstiltskin   140

Story of the Youth Who Went Forth to Learn What Fear Was   146

Little Snow-White   162

Cinderella   176

Godfather Death   188

The Golden Goose   194

The Story of Schlauraffenland   202

Hansel & Grethel

Illustrated by Judith Zaugg

Hard by a great forest dwelt a poor wood-cutter with his wife and his two children. The boy was called Hansel and the girl Grethel. He had little to bite and to break, and once when great scarcity fell on the land, he could no longer procure daily bread. Now when he thought over this by night in his bed, and tossed about in his anxiety, he groaned and said to his wife: "What is to become of us? How are we to feed our poor children, when we no longer have anything even for ourselves?" "I'll tell you what, husband," answered the woman, "early tomorrow morning we will take the children out into the forest to where it is the thickest, there we will light a fire for them, and give each of them one piece of bread more, and then we will go to our work and leave them alone. They will not find the way home again, and we shall be rid of them." — "No, wife," said the man, "I will not do that; how can I bear to leave my children alone in the forest? The wild animals would soon come and tear them to pieces." — "O, thou fool!" said she, "then we must all four die of hunger, thou mayest as well plane the planks for our coffins," and she left him no peace until he consented. "But I feel very sorry for the poor children, all the same," said the man.

The two children had also not been able to sleep for hunger, and had heard what their step-mother had said to their father. Grethel wept bitter tears, and said to Hansel: "Now all is over with us." — "Be quiet, Grethel," said Hansel, "do not distress thyself, I will soon find a way to help us." And when the old folks had fallen asleep, he got up, put on his little coat, opened the door below, and crept outside. The moon shone brightly, and the white pebbles which lay in front of the house glittered like real silver pennies. Hansel stooped and put as many of them in the little pocket of his coat as he could possibly get in. Then he went back and said to

Grethel: "Be comforted, dear little sister, and sleep in peace, God will not forsake us," and he lay down again in his bed. When day dawned, but before the sun had risen, the woman came and awoke the two children, saying "Get up, you sluggards! we are going into the forest to fetch wood." She gave each a little piece of bread, and said: "There is something for your dinner, but do not eat it up before then, for you will get nothing else." Grethel took the bread under her apron, as Hansel had the stones in his pocket. Then they all set out together on the way to the forest. When they had walked a short time, Hansel stood still and peeped back at the house, and did so again and again. His father said: "Hansel, what art thou looking at there and staying behind for? Mind what thou art about, and do not forget how to use thy legs." — "Ah, father," said Hansel, "I am looking at my little white cat, which is sitting up on the roof, and wants to say good-bye to me." The wife said: "Fool, that is not thy little cat, that is the morning sun which is shining on the chimneys." Hansel, however, had not been looking back at the cat, but had been constantly throwing one of the white pebble-stones out of his pocket on the road. When they had reached the middle of the forest, the father said: "Now, children, pile up some wood, and I will light a fire that you may not be cold." Hansel and Grethel gathered brushwood together, as high as a little hill. The brushwood was lighted, and when the flames were burning very high, the woman said: "Now, children, lay yourselves down by the fire and rest, we will go into the forest and cut some wood. When we have done, we will come back and fetch you away."

Hansel and Grethel sat by the fire, and when noon came, each ate a little piece of bread, and as they heard the strokes of the wood-axe they believed that their father was near. It was not, however, the axe, it was a branch which he had fastened to a withered tree which the wind was blowing backwards and forwards. And as they had been sitting such a long time, their eyes shut with fatigue, and they fell fast asleep. When at last they awoke, it was already dark night. Grethel began to cry and said: "How are we to get out of the forest now?" But Hansel comforted her and said: "Just wait a little, until the moon has risen, and then we will soon find the way." And when the full moon had risen, Hansel took his little sister by the hand, and followed the pebbles which shone like newly-coined silver pieces, and showed them the way.

They walked the whole night long, and by break of day came once more to their father's house. They knocked at the door, and when the woman opened it and saw that it was Hansel and Grethel, she said: "You naughty children, why have you slept so long in the forest? We thought you were never coming back at all!" The father, however, rejoiced, for it had cut him to the heart to leave them behind alone.

Not long afterwards, there was once more great scarcity in all parts, and the children heard their mother saying at night to their father: "Everything is eaten again, we have one half loaf left, and after that there is an end. The children must go, we will take them farther into the wood, so that they will not find their way out again; there is no other means of saving ourselves!" The man's heart was heavy, and he thought "it would be better for thee to share the last mouthful with thy children." The woman, however, would listen to nothing that he had to say, but scolded and reproached him. He who says A must say B, likewise, and as he had yielded the first time, he had to do so a second time also.

The children were, however, still awake and had heard the conversation. When the old folks were asleep, Hansel again got up, and wanted to go out and pick up pebbles as he had done before, but the woman had locked the door, and Hansel could not get out. Nevertheless he comforted his little sister, and said: "Do not cry, Grethel, go to sleep quietly, the good God will help us."

Early in the morning came the woman, and took the children out of their beds. Their bit of bread was given to them, but it was still smaller than the time before. On the way into the forest Hansel crumbled his in his pocket, and often stood still and threw a morsel on the ground. "Hansel, why dost thou stop and look round?" said the father, "go on." — "I am looking back at my little pigeon which is sitting on the roof, and wants to say good-bye to me," answered Hansel. "Simpleton!" said the woman, "that is not thy little pigeon, that is the morning sun that is shining on the chimney." Hansel, however, little by little, threw all the crumbs on the path. The woman led the children still deeper into the forest, where they had never in their lives been before. Then a great fire was again made, and the mother said: "Just sit there, you children, and when you are tired you may sleep a little; we are going into the forest to cut wood, and in the evening when we are done, we will come and fetch you away." When it was noon, Grethel shared her piece of bread

with Hansel, who had scattered his by the way. Then they fell asleep and evening came and went, but no one came to the poor children. They did not awake until it was dark night, and Hansel comforted his little sister and said: "Just wait, Grethel, until the moon rises, and then we shall see the crumbs of bread which I have strewn about, they will show us our way home again." When the moon came they set out, but they found no crumbs, for the many thousands of birds which fly about in the woods and fields had picked them all up. Hansel said to Grethel: "We shall soon find the way," but they did not find it. They walked the whole night and all the next day too from morning till evening, but they did not get out of the forest, and were very hungry, for they had nothing to eat but two or three berries, which grew on the ground. And as they were so weary that their legs would carry them no longer, they lay down beneath a tree and fell asleep.

It was now three mornings since they had left their father's house. They began to walk again, but they always got deeper into the forest, and if help did not come soon, they must die of hunger and weariness. When it was mid-day, they saw a beautiful snow-white bird sitting on a bough, which sang so delightfully that they stood still and listened to it. And when it had finished its song, it spread its wings and flew away before them, and they followed it until they reached a little house, on the roof of which it alighted; and when they came quite up to little house they saw that it was built of bread and covered with cakes, but that the windows were of clear sugar. "We will set to work on that," said Hansel, "and have a good meal. I will eat a bit of the roof, and thou, Grethel, canst eat some of the window, it will taste sweet." Hansel reached up above, and broke off a little of the roof to try how it tasted, and Grethel leant against the window and nibbled at the panes. Then a soft voice cried from the room:

"Nibble, nibble, gnaw, who is nibbling at my little house?"

The children answered: "The wind, the wind, the heaven-born wind,"

and went on eating without disturbing themselves. Hansel, who thought the roof tasted very nice, tore down a great piece of it, and Grethel pushed out the whole of one round window-pane, sat down, and enjoyed herself with it. Suddenly the door opened, and a very, very old woman, who supported herself on crutches, came creeping out. Hansel and Grethel were so terribly frightened that they let fall what they had in their hands. The old woman, however, nodded her head, and said: "Oh, you dear children, who has brought you here? Do come in, and stay with me. No harm shall happen to you." She took them both by the hand, and led them into her little house. Then good food was set before them, milk and pancakes, with sugar, apples, and nuts. Afterwards two pretty little beds were covered with clean white linen, and Hansel and Grethel lay down in them, and thought they were in heaven.

The old woman had only pretended to be so kind; she was in reality a wicked witch, who lay in wait for children, and had only built the little house of bread in order to entice them there. When a child fell into her power, she killed it, cooked and ate it, and that was a feast day with her. Witches have red eyes, and cannot see far, but they have a keen scent like the beasts, and are aware when human beings draw near. When Hansel and Grethel came into her neighborhood, she laughed maliciously, and said mockingly: "I have them, they shall not escape me again!"

Early in the morning before the children were awake, she was already up, and when she saw both of them sleeping and looking so pretty, with their plump red cheeks, she muttered to herself: "That will be a dainty mouthful!" Then she seized Hansel with her shrivelled hand, carried him into a little stable, and shut him in with a grated door. He might scream as he liked, that was of no use. Then she went to Grethel, shook her till she awoke, and cried: "Get up, lazy thing, fetch some water, and cook something good for thy brother, he is in the stable outside, and is to be made fat. When he is fat, I will eat him." Grethel began to weep bitterly, but it was all in vain, she was forced to do what the wicked witch ordered her.

And now the best food was cooked for poor Hansel, but Grethel got nothing but crab-shells. Every morning the woman crept to the little stable, and cried: "Hansel, stretch out thy finger that I may feel if thou wilt soon be fat." Hansel, however, stretched out a little bone to her, and the old woman, who had dim eyes, could not see it, and thought it was Hansel's finger, and was astonished that there was no way of fattening him. When four weeks had gone by, and Hansel still continued thin, she was seized with impatience and would not wait any longer. "Hola, Grethel," she cried to the girl, "be active, and bring some water. Let Hansel be fat or lean, tomorrow I will kill him, and cook him." Ah, how the poor little sister did lament when she had to fetch the water, and how her tears did flow down over her cheeks! "Dear God, do help us," she cried. "If the wild beasts in the forest had but devoured us, we should at any rate have died together." — "Just keep thy noise to thyself," said the old woman, "all that won't help thee at all."

Early in the morning, Grethel had to go out and hang up the cauldron with the water, and light the fire. "We will bake first," said the old woman, "I have already heated the oven, and kneaded the dough." She pushed poor Grethel out to the oven, from which flames of fire were already darting. "Creep in," said the witch, "and see if it is properly heated, so that we can shut the bread in." And when once Grethel was inside, she intended to shut the oven and let her bake in it, and then she would eat her, too. But Grethel saw what she had in her mind, and said: "I do not know how I am to do it; how do you get in?" — "Silly goose," said the old woman, "the door is big enough; just look, I can get in myself!" and she crept up and thrust her head into the oven. Then Grethel gave her a push that drove her far into it, and shut the iron door, and fastened the bolt. Oh! then she began to howl quite horribly, but Grethel ran away, and the godless witch was miserably burnt to death.

Grethel, however, ran like lightning to Hansel, opened his little stable, and cried: "Hansel, we are saved! The old witch is dead!" Then Hansel sprang out like a bird from its cage when the door is opened for it. How they did rejoice and embrace each other, and dance about and kiss each other! And as they had no longer any need to fear her, they went into the witch's house, and in every corner there stood chests full of pearls and jewels. "These are far better than pebbles!" said Hansel, and thrust into his pockets whatever could be got in, and Grethel said, "I, too, will take something home with me," and filled her pinafore full. "But now we will go away," said Hansel, "that we may get out of the witch's forest."

When they had walked for two hours, they came to a great piece of water. "We cannot get over," said Hansel, "I see no foot-plank, and no bridge." — "And no boat crosses either," answered Grethel, "but a white duck is swimming there; if I ask her, she will help us over." Then she cried,

"Little duck, little duck, dost thou see,
Hansel and Grethel are waiting for thee?
There's never a plank, or bridge in sight,
Take us across on thy back so white."

The duck came to them, and Hansel seated himself on its back, and told his sister to sit by him. "No," replied Grethel, "that will be too heavy for the little duck; she shall take us across, one after the other." The good little duck did so, and when they were once safely across and had walked for a short time, the forest seemed to be more and more familiar to them, and at length they saw from afar their father's house. Then they began to run, rushed into the parlour, and threw themselves into their father's arms. The man had not known one happy hour since he had left the children in the forest; the woman, however, was dead. Grethel emptied her pinafore until pearls and precious stones ran about the room, and Hansel threw one handful after another out of his pocket to add to them. Then all anxiety was at an end, and they lived together in perfect happiness. My tale is done, there runs a mouse, whosoever catches it, may make himself a big fur cap out of it.

18

Little Red-Cap

Illustrated by Rilla Alexander

Once upon a time there was a dear little girl who was loved by every one who looked at her, but most of all by her grandmother, and there was nothing that she would not have given to the child. Once she gave her a little cap of red velvet, which suited her so well that she would never wear anything else; so she was always called "Little Red-Cap."

One day her mother said to her: "Come, Little Red-Cap, here is a piece of cake and a bottle of wine; take them to your grandmother, she is ill and weak, and they will do her good. Set out before it gets hot, and when you are going, walk nicely and quietly and do not run off the path, or you may fall and break the bottle, and then your grandmother will get nothing; and when you go into her room, don't forget to say, 'Good-morning,' and don't peep into every corner before you do it."

"I will take great care," said Little Red-Cap to her mother, and gave her hand on it. The grandmother lived out in the wood, half a league from the village, and just as Little Red-Cap entered the wood, a wolf met her. Red-Cap did not know what a wicked creature he was, and was not at all afraid of him.

"Good-day, Little Red-Cap," said he. - "Thank you kindly, wolf." — "Whither away so early, Little Red-Cap?" — "To my grandmother's." — "What have you got in your apron?" — "Cake and wine; yesterday was baking-day, so poor sick grandmother is to have something good, to make her stronger." — "Where does your grandmother live, Little Red-Cap?" — "A good quarter of a league farther on in the wood; her house stands under the three large oak-trees, the nut-trees are just below; you surely must know it," replied Little Red-Cap. The wolf thought to himself: "What a tender young creature! what a nice plump mouthful – she will be better to eat than the old woman. I must act craftily, so as to catch both." So he walked for a short time by the side of Little Red-Cap, and then he said: "See Little Red-Cap, how pretty the flowers are about here – why do you not look round? I believe, too, that you do not hear how sweetly the little birds are singing; you walk gravely along as if you were going to school, while everything else out here in the wood is merry."

Little Red-Cap raised her éyes, and when she saw the sunbeams dancing here and there through the trees, and pretty flowers growing everywhere, she thought: "Suppose I take grandmother a fresh nosegay; that would please her too. It is so early in the day that I shall still get there in good time." And so she ran from the path into the wood to look for flowers. And whenever she had picked one, she fancied that she saw a still prettier one farther on, and ran after it, and so got deeper and deeper into the wood.

Meanwhile the wolf ran straight to the grandmother's house and knocked at the door. "Who is there?" — "Little Red-Cap," replied the wolf. "She is bringing cake and wine; open the door." — "Lift the latch," called out the grandmother, "I am too weak, and cannot get up." The wolf lifted the latch, the door flew open, and without saying a word he went straight to the grandmother's bed, and devoured her. Then he put on her clothes, dressed himself in her cap, laid himself in bed and drew the curtains.

Little Red-Cap, however, had been running about picking flowers, and when she had gathered so many that she could carry no more, she remembered her grandmother, and set out on the way to her. She was surprised to find the cottage-door standing open, and when she went into the room, she had such a strange feeling that she said to herself: "Oh dear! how uneasy I feel to-day, and at other times I like being with grandmother so much." She called out: "Good morning," but received no answer; so she went to the bed and drew back the curtains. There lay her grandmother with her cap pulled far over her face, and looking very strange. "Oh! grandmother," she said, "what big ears you have!"

"The better to hear you with, my child," was the reply. "But, grandmother, what big eyes you have!" she said. — "The better to see you with, my dear." — "But, grandmother, what large hands you have!" — "The better to hug you with."

"Oh! but, grandmother, what a terrible big mouth you have!" — "The better to eat you with!" And scarcely had the wolf said this, than with one bound he was out of bed and swallowed up Red-Cap.

When the wolf had appeased his appetite, he lay down again in the bed, fell asleep and began to snore very loud. The huntsman was just passing the house, and thought to himself: "How the old woman is snoring! I must just see if she wants anything." So he went into the room, and when he came to the bed, he saw that the wolf was lying in it. "Do I find thee here, thou old sinner!" said he. "I have long sought thee!" Then just as he was going to fire at him, it occurred to him that the wolf might have devoured the grandmother, and that she might still be saved, so he did not fire, but took a pair of scissors, and began to cut open the stomach of the sleeping wolf. When he had made two snips, he saw the little Red-Cap shining, and then he made two snips more, and the little girl sprang out, crying: "Ah, how frightened I have been! How dark it was inside the wolf!" and after that the aged grandmother came out alive also, but scarcely able to breathe. Red-Cap, however, quickly fetched great stones with which they filled the wolf's body, and when he awoke, he wanted to run away; but the stones were so heavy that he fell down at once, and fell dead. Then all three were delighted. The huntsman drew off the wolf's skin and went home with it; the grandmother ate the cake and drank the wine which Red-Cap had brought, and revived, but Red-Cap thought to herself: "As long as I live, I will never by myself leave the path, to run into the wood, when my mother has forbidden me to do so."

24

The Frog-King

Illustrated by Michał Książek

In old times when wishing still helped one, there lived a king whose daughters were all beautiful, but the youngest was so beautiful that the sun itself, which has seen so much, was astonished whenever it shone in her face. Close by the King's castle lay a great dark forest, and under an old lime-tree in the forest was a well, and when the day was very warm, the King's child went out into the forest and sat down by the side of the cool fountain, and when she was dull she took a golden ball, and threw it up on high and caught it, and this ball was her favorite plaything.

Now it so happened that on one occasion the princess's golden ball did not fall into the little hand which she was holding up for it, but on to the ground beyond, and rolled straight into the water. The King's daughter followed it with her eyes, but it vanished, and the well was deep, so deep that the bottom could not be seen. On this she began to cry, and cried louder and louder, and could not be comforted.

And as she thus lamented some one said to her: "What ails thee, King's daughter? Thou weepest so that even a stone would show pity." She looked round to the side from whence the voice came, and saw a frog stretching forth its thick, ugly head from the water. "Ah! Old water-splasher, is it thou?" said she; "I am weeping for my golden ball, which has fallen into the well." — "Be quiet, and do not weep," answered the frog, "I can help thee, but what wilt thou give me if I bring thy plaything up again?" — "Whatever thou wilt have, dear frog," said she; "My clothes, my pearls and jewels, and even the golden crown which I am wearing." The frog answered: "I do not care for thy clothes, thy pearls and jewels, or thy golden crown, but if thou wilt love me and let me be thy companion and play-fellow, and sit by thee at thy little table, and eat off thy little golden plate, and drink out of thy little cup, and sleep in thy little bed – if thou wilt promise me this I will go down below, and bring thee thy golden ball up again." — "Oh yes," said she, "I promise thee all thou wishest, if thou wilt but bring me my ball back again." She, however, thought: "How the silly frog does talk! He lives in the water with the other frogs, and croaks, and can be no companion to any human being!"

But the frog when he had received this promise, put his head into the water and sank down, and in a short while came swimmming up again with the ball in his mouth, and threw it on the grass. The King's daughter was delighted to see her pretty plaything once more, and picked it up, and ran away with it. "Wait, wait," said the frog. "Take me with thee. I can't run as thou canst." But what did it avail him to scream his croak, croak, after her, as loudly as he could? She did not listen to it, but ran home and soon forgot the poor frog, who was forced to go back into his well again.

The next day when she had seated herself at table with the King and all the courtiers, and was eating from her little golden plate, something came creeping splish splash, splish splash, up the marble staircase, and when it had got to the top, it knocked at the door and cried:

"Princess, youngest princess, open the door for me."

She ran to see who was outside, but when she opened the door, there sat the frog in front of it. Then she slammed the door to, in great haste, sat down to dinner again, and was quite frightened. The King saw plainly that her heart was beating violently, and said: "My child, what art thou so afraid of? Is there perchance a giant outside who wants to carry thee away?" — "Ah, no," replied she. "It is no giant but a disgusting frog."
"What does a frog want with thee?" — "Ah, dear father, yesterday as I was in the forest sitting by the well, playing, my golden ball fell into the water. And because I cried so, the frog brought it out again for me, and because he so insisted, I promised him he should be my companion, but I never thought he would be able to come out of his water! And now he is outside there, and wants to come in to me."

In the meantime it knocked a second time, and cried:

"Princess! youngest princess! Open the door for me!
Dost thou not know what thou saidst to me
Yesterday by the cool waters of the fountain?
Princess, youngest princess! Open the door for me!"

Then said the King: "That which thou hast promised must thou perform. Go and let him in." She went and opened the door, and the frog hopped in and followed her, step by step, to her chair. There he sat and cried: "Lift me up beside thee." She delayed, until at last the King commanded her to do it. When the frog was once on the chair he wanted to be on the table, and when he was on the table he said: "Now, push thy little golden plate nearer to me that we may eat together." She did this, but it was easy to see that she did not do it willingly. The frog enjoyed what he ate, but almost every mouthful she took choked her. At length he said: "I have eaten and am satisfied; now I am tired, carry me into thy little room

28

and make thy little silken bed ready, and we will both lie down and go to sleep."
The King's daughter began to cry, for she was afraid of the cold frog which she did
not like to touch, and which was now to sleep in her pretty, clean little bed. But
the King grew angry and said: "He who helped thee when thou wert in trouble
ought not afterwards to be despised by thee." So she took hold of the frog with
two fingers, carried him upstairs, and put him in a corner. But when she was in
bed he crept to her and said: "I am tired, I want to sleep as well as thou, lift me up
or I will tell thy father." Then she was terribly angry, and took him up and threw
him with all her might against the wall. "Now, thou wilt be quiet, odious frog,"
said she. But when he fell down he was no frog but a King's son with beautiful
kind eyes. He by her father's will was now her dear companion and husband.
Then he told her how he had been bewitched by a wicked witch, and how no one
could have delivered him from the well but herself, and that to-morrow they
would go together into his kingdom. Then they went to sleep, and next morning
when the sun awoke them, a carriage came driving up with eight white horses,
which had white ostrich feathers on their heads, and were harnessed with golden

chains, and behind stood the young King's servant Faithful Henry. Faithful Henry had been so unhappy when his master was changed into a frog, that he had caused three iron bands to be laid round his heart, lest it should burst with grief and sadness. The carriage was to conduct the young King into his Kingdom. Faithful Henry helped them both in, and placed himself behind again, and was full of joy because of this deliverance. And when they had driven a part of the way the King's son heard a cracking behind him as if something had broken. So he turned round and cried: "Henry, the carriage is breaking."

"No, master, it is not the carriage,
It is a band from my heart,
Which was put there in my great pain
When you were a frog and imprisoned in the well."

Again and once again while they were on their way something cracked, and each time the King's son thought the carriage was breaking; but it was only the bands which were springing from the heart of Faithful Henry because his master was set free and was happy.

King Thrushbeard

Illustrated by Christian Montenegro

A King had a daughter who was beautiful beyond all measure, but so proud and haughty withal that no suitor was good enough for her. She sent away one after the other, and ridiculed them as well.

Once the King made a great feast and invited thereto, from far and near, all the young men likely to marry. They were all marshalled in a row according to their rank and standing; first came the kings, then the grand-dukes, then the princes, the earls, the barons, and the gentry. Then the King's daughter was led through the ranks, but to every one she had some objection to make; one was too fat: "The wine-cask," she said. Another was too tall: "Long and thin has little in." The third was too short: "Short and thick is never quick." The fourth was too pale: "As pale as death." The fifth too red: "A fighting-cock." The sixth was not straight enough: "A green log dried behind the stove."

So she had something to say against every one, but she made herself especially merry over a good king who stood quite high up in the row, and whose chin had grown a little crooked. "Well," she cried and laughed, "he has a chin like a thrush's beak!" and from that time he got the name of King Thrushbeard.

But the old King, when he saw that his daugher did nothing but mock the people, and despised all the suitors who were gathered there, was very angry, and swore that she should have for her husband the very first beggar that came to his doors. A few days afterwards a fiddler came and sang beneath the windows, trying to earn a small alms. When the King heard him he said: "Let him come up." So the fiddler came in, in his dirty, ragged clothes, and sang before the King and his daughter, and when he had ended he asked for a trifling gift. The King said: "Your song has pleased me so well that I will give you my daughter there, to wife."

The King's daughter shuddered, but the King said: "I have taken an oath to give you to the very first beggar-man, and I will keep it." All she could say was in vain; the priest was brought, and she had to let herself be wedded to the fiddler on the spot. When that was done the King said: "Now it is not proper for you, a beggar-woman, to stay any longer in my palace, you may just go away with your husband." The beggar-man led her out by the hand, and she was obliged to walk away on foot with him.

When they came to a large forest she asked: "To whom does that beautiful forest belong?" — "It belongs to King Thrushbeard; if you had taken him, it would have been yours." — "Ah, unhappy girl that I am, if I had but taken King Thrushbeard!" Afterwards they came to a meadow, and she asked again: "To whom does this beautiful green meadow belong?" — "It belongs to King Thrushbeard; if you had taken him, it would have been yours." — "Ah, unhappy girl that I am, if I had but taken King Thrushbeard!"

Then they came to a large town, and she asked again: "To whom does this fine large town belong?" — "It belongs to King Thrushbeard; if you had taken him, it would have been yours." — "Ah, unhappy girl that I am, if I had but taken King Thrushbeard!"

"It does not please me," said the fiddler, "to hear you always wishing for another husband; am I not good enough for you?" At last they came to a very little hut, and she said: "Oh goodness! what a small house; to whom does this miserable, mean hovel belong?" The fiddler answered: "That is my house and yours, where we shall live together."

She had to stoop in order to go in at the low door. "Where are the servants?" said the King's daughter. "What servants?" answered the beggar-man; "you must yourself do what you wish to have done. Just make a fire at once, and set on water to cook my supper, I am quite tired." But the King's daughter knew nothing about lighting fires or cooking, and the beggar-man had to lend a hand himself to get anything fairly done. When they had finished their scanty meal they went to bed; but he forced her to get up quite early in the morning in order to look after the house.

For a few days they lived in this way as well as might be, and came to the end of all their provisions. Then the man said: "Wife, we cannot go on any longer eating and drinking here and earning nothing. You weave baskets." He went out, cut

35

some willows, and brought them home. Then she began to weave, but the tough willows wounded her delicate hands.

"I see that this will not do," said the man; "you had better spin, perhaps you can do that better." She sat down and tried to spin, but the hard thread soon cut her soft fingers so that the blood ran down. "See," said the man, "you are fit for no sort of work; I have made a bad bargain with you. Now I will try to make a business with pots and earthenware; you must sit in the market-place and sell the ware." "Alas," thought she, "if any of the people from my father's kingdom come to the market and see me sitting there, selling, how they will mock me?" But it was of no use, she had to yield unless she chose to die of hunger.

For the first time she succeeded well, for the people were glad to buy the woman's wares because she was good-looking, and they paid her what she asked; many even gave her the money and left the pots with her as well. So they lived on what she had earned as long as it lasted, then the husband bought a lot of new crockery. With this she sat down at the corner of the market-place, and set it out round about her ready for sale. But suddenly there came a drunken hussar galloping

36

along, and he rode right amongst the pots so that they were all broken into a thousand bits. She began to weep, and did now know what to do for fear. "Alas! what will happen to me?" cried she; "what will my husband say to this?" She ran home and told him of the misfortune. "Who would seat herself at a corner of the market-place with crockery?" said the man; "leave off crying, I see very well that you cannot do any ordinary work, so I have been to our King's palace and have asked whether they cannot find a place for a kitchen-maid, and they have promised me to take you; in that way you will get your food for nothing."

The King's daughter was now a kitchen-maid, and had to be at the cook's beck and call, and do the dirtiest work. In both her pockets she fastened a little jar, in which she took home her share of the leavings, and upon this they lived. It happened that the wedding of the King's eldest son was to be celebrated, so the poor woman went up and placed herself by the door of the hall to look on. When all the candles were lit, and people, each more beautiful than the other, entered, and all was full of pomp and splendour, she thought of her lot with a sad heart, and cursed the pride and haughtiness which had humbled her and brought her to so great poverty.

The smell of the delicious dishes which were being taken in and out reached her, and now and then the servants threw her a few morsels of them: these she put in her jars to take home.

All at once the King's son entered, clothed in velvet and silk, with gold chains about his neck. And when he saw the beautiful woman standing by the door he seized her by the hand, and would have danced with her; but she refused and shrank with fear, for she saw that it was King Thrushbeard, her suitor whom she had driven away with scorn. Her struggles were of no avail, he drew her into the hall; but the string by which her pockets were hung broke, the pots fell down, the soup ran out, and the scraps were scattered all about. And when the people saw it, there arose general laughter and derision, and she was so ashamed that she would rather have been a thousand fathoms below the ground. She sprang to the door and would have run away, but on the stairs a man caught her and brought her back; and when she looked at him it was King Thrushbeard again. He said to her kindly: "Do not be afraid, I and the fiddler who has been living with you in that wretched hovel are one. For love of you I disguised myself so; and I also was the hussar who rode through your crockery. This was all done to humble your proud spirit, and to punish you for the insolence with which you mocked me."

Then she wept bitterly and said: "I have done great wrong, and am not worthy to be your wife." But he said: "Be comforted, the evil days are past; now we will celebrate our wedding." Then the maids-in-waiting came and put on her the most splendid clothing, and her father and his whole court came and wished her happiness in her marriage with King Thrushbeard, and the joy now began in earnest. I wish you and I had been there too.

The Bremen Town-Musicians

Illustrated by Koshiro Torisu

A certain man had a donkey, which had carried the corn-sacks to the mill inde-fatigably for many a long year; but his strength was going, and he was growing more and more unfit for work. Then his master began to consider how he might best save his keep; but the donkey, seeing that no good wind was blowing, ran away and set out on the road to Bremen. "There," he thought, "I can surely be town-musician." When he had walked some distance, he found a hound lying on the road, gasping like one who had run till he was tired. "What are you gasping so for, you big fellow?" asked the donkey.

"Ah," replied the hound, "as I am old, and daily grow weaker, and no longer can hunt, my master wanted to kill me, so I took to flight; but now how am I to earn my bread?"

"I tell you what," said the donkey, "I am going to Bremen, and shall be town-mu-sician there; go with me and engage yourself also as a musician. I will play the lute, and you shall beat the kettledrum." The hound agreed, and on they went.

Before long they came to a cat, sitting on the path, with a face like three rainy days! "Now then, old shaver, what has gone askew with you?" asked the donkey. "Who can be merry when his neck is in danger?" answered the cat. "Because I am now getting old, and my teeth are worn to stumps, and I prefer to sit by the fire and spin, rather than hunt about after mice, my mistress wanted to drown me, so I ran away. But now good advice is scarce. Where am I to go?"

"Go with us to Bremen. You understand night-music, you can be a town-musician." The cat thought well of it, and went with them. After this the three fugitives came to a farm-yard, where the cock was sitting upon the gate, crowing with all his might. "Your crow goes through and through one," said the donkey. "What is the matter?"

"I have been foretelling fine weather, because it is the day on which Our Lady washes the Christ-child's little shirts, and wants to dry them," said the cock; "but guests are coming for Sunday, so the housewife has no pity, and has told the cook that she intends to eat me in the soup to-morrow, and this evening I am to have my head cut off. Now I am crowing at full pitch while I can."

"Ah, but red-comb," said the donkey, "you had better come away with us. We are going to Bremen; you can find something better than death everywhere: you have a good voice, and if we make music together it must have some quality!"

The cock agreed to this plan, and all four went on together. They could not, however, reach the city of Bremen in one day, and in the evening they came to a forest where they meant to pass the night. The donkey and the hound laid themselves down under a large tree, the cat and the cock settled themselves in the branches; but the cock flew right to the top, where he was most safe. Before he went to sleep he looked round on all four sides, and thought he saw in the distance a little spark burning; so he called out to his companions that there must be a house not far off, for he saw a light. The donkey said: "If so, we had better get up and go on, for the shelter here is bad." The hound thought that a few bones with some meat on would do him good too!

So they made their way to the place where the light was, and soon saw it shine brighter and grow larger, until they came to a well-lighted robber's house. The donkey, as the biggest, went to the window and looked in.

"What do you see, my grey-horse?" asked the cock. "What do I see?" answered the donkey; "a table covered with good things to eat and drink, and robbers sitting at it enjoying themselves." — "That would be the sort of thing for us," said the cock. "Yes, yes; ah, how I wish we were there!" said the donkey.

Then the animals took counsel together how they should manage to drive away the robbers, and at last they thought of a plan. The donkey was to place himself with his fore-feet upon the window-ledge, the hound was to jump on the donkey's back, the cat was to climb upon the dog, and lastly the cock was to fly up and perch upon the head of the cat.

When this was done, at a given signal, they began to perform their music together: the donkey brayed, the hound barked, the cat mewed, and the cock crowed; then they burst through the window into the room, so that the glass clattered! At this horrible din, the robbers sprang up, thinking no otherwise than that a ghost had come in, and fled in a great fright out into the forest. The four companions now sat down at the table, well content with what was left, and ate as if they were going to fast for a month.

As soon as the four minstrels had done, they put out the light, and each sought for himself a sleeping-place according to his nature and to what suited him. The donkey laid himself down upon some straw in the yard, the hound behind the door, the cat upon the hearth near the warm ashes, and the cock perched himself upon a beam of the roof; and being tired from their long walk, they soon went to sleep. When it was past midnight, and the robbers saw from afar that the light was no longer burning in their house, and all appeared quiet, the captain said: "We ought not to have let ourselves be frightened out of our wits;" and ordered one of them to go and examine the house.

The messenger finding all still, went into the kitchen to light a candle, and, taking the glistening fiery eyes of the cat for live coals, he held a lucifer-match to them

44

to light it. But the cat did not understand the joke, and flew in his face, spitting and scratching. He was dreadfully frightened, and ran to the back-door, but the dog, who lay there sprang up and bit his leg; and as he ran across the yard by the straw-heap, the donkey gave him a smart kick with its hind foot. The cock, too, who had been awakened by the noise, and had become lively, cried down from the beam: "Cock-a-doodle-doo!"

Then the robber ran back as fast as he could to his captain, and said: "Ah, there is a horrible witch sitting in the house, who spat on me and scratched my face with her long claws; and by the door stands a man with a knife, who stabbed me in the leg; and in the yard there lies a black monster, who beat me with a wooden club; and above, upon the roof, sits the judge, who called out, 'Bring the rogue here to me!' so I got away as well as I could."

After this the robbers did not trust themselves in the house again; but it suited the four musicians of Bremen so well that they did not care to leave it any more. And the mouth of him who last told this story is still warm.

Hans in Luck

Illustrated by Koraters

Hans had served his master for seven years, so he said to him: "Master, my time is up; now I should be glad to go back home to my mother; give me my wages." The master answered: "You have served me faithfully and honestly; as the service was so shall the reward be;" and he gave Hans a piece of gold as big as his head. Hans pulled his handkerchief out of his pocket, wrapped up the lump in it, put it on his shoulder, and set out on the way home.

As he went on, always putting one foot before the other, he saw a horseman trotting quickly and merrily by on a lively horse. "Ah!" said Hans quite loud, "what a fine thing it is to ride! There you sit as on a chair; you stumble over no stones, you save your shoes, and get on, you don't know how."

The rider, who had heard him, stopped and called out: "Hollo! Hans, why do you go on foot, then?" — "I must," answered he, "for I have this lump to carry home; it is true that it is gold, but I cannot hold my head straight for it, and it hurts my shoulder." — "I will tell you what," said the rider, "we will exchange: I will give you my horse, and you can give me your lump." — "With all my heart," said Hans, "but I can tell you, you will have to crawl along with it."

The rider got down, took the gold, and helped Hans up; then gave him the bridle tight in his hands and said: "If you want to go at a really good pace, you must click your tongue and call out: 'Jup! Jup!'"

Hans was heartily delighted as he sat upon the horse and rode away so bold and free. After a little while he thought that it ought to go faster, and he began to click with his tongue and call out: "Jup! Jup!" The horse put himself into a sharp trot, and before Hans knew where he was, he was thrown off and lying in a ditch which separated the field from the highway. The horse would have gone off too if it had not been stopped by a countryman, who was coming along the road and driving a cow before him.

Hans got his limbs together and stood up on his legs again, but he was vexed, and said to the countryman: "It is a poor joke, this riding, especially when one gets hold of a mare like this, that kicks and throws one off, so that one has a chance of breaking one's neck. Never again will I mount it. Now I like your cow, for one can walk quietly behind her, and have, over and above, one's milk, butter and cheese every day without fail. What would I not give to have such a cow." "Well," said the countryman, "if it would give you so much pleasure, I do not mind giving the cow for the horse." Hans agreed with the greatest delight; the countryman jumped upon the horse, and rode quickly away.

Hans drove his cow quietly before him, and thought over his lucky bargain. "If only I have a morsel of bread – and that can hardly fail me – I can eat butter and cheese with it as often as I like; if I am thirsty, I can milk my cow and drink the milk. Good heart, what more can I want?" When he came to an inn he made a halt, and in his great content ate up what he had with him – his dinner and supper –

and all he had, and with his last few farthings had half a glass of beer. Then he drove his cow onwards along the road to his mother's village.

As it drew nearer mid-day, the heat was more oppressive, and Hans found himself upon a moor which it took about an hour to cross. He felt it very hot and his tongue clave to the roof of his mouth with thirst. "I can find a cure for this," thought Hans; "I will milk the cow now and refresh myself with the milk." He tied her to a withered tree, and as he had no pail he put his leather cap underneath; but try as he would, not a drop of milk came. And as he set himself to work in a clumsy way, the impatient beast at last gave him such a blow on his head with its hind foot, that he fell on the ground, and for a long time could not think where he was.

By good fortune a butcher just then came along the road with a wheel-barrow, in which lay a young pig. "What sort of a trick is this?" cried he, and helped the good Hans up. Hans told him what had happened. The butcher gave him his flask and said: "Take a drink and refresh yourself. The cow will certainly give no milk, it is an old beast; at the best it is only fit for the plough, or for the butcher." — "Well, well," said Hans, as he stroked his hair down on his head, "who would have thought it? Certainly it is a fine thing when one can kill a beast like that at home; what meat one has! But I do not care much for beef, it is not juicy enough for me. A young pig like that now is the thing to have, it tastes quite different; and then there are the sausages!" - "Hark ye, Hans," said the butcher, "out of love for you I will exchange, and will let you have the pig for the cow." — "Heaven repay you for your kindness!" said Hans as he gave up the cow, whilst the pig was unbound from the barrow, and the cord by which it was tied was put in his hand.

Hans went on, and thought to himself how everything was going just as he wished; if he did meet with any vexation it was immediately set right. Presently there joined him a lad who was carrying a fine white goose under his arm. They said good morning to each other, and Hans began to tell of his good luck, and how he had always made such good bargains. The boy told him that he was taking the goose to a christening-feast. "Just lift her," added he, and laid hold of her by the wings; "how heavy she is – she has been fattened up for the last eight weeks. Whoever has a bit of her when she is roasted will have to wipe the fat from both sides of his mouth." — "Yes," said Hans, as he weighed her in one hand, "she is a good weight, but my pig is no bad one."

Meanwhile the lad looked suspiciously from one side to the other, and shook his head. "Look here," he said at length, "it may not be all right with your pig. In the village through which I passed, the Mayor himself had just had one stolen out of its sty. I fear – I fear that you have got hold of it there. They have sent out some people and it would be a bad business if they caught you with the pig; at the very least, you would be shut up in the dark hole."

The good Hans was terrified. "Goodness!" he said, "help me out of this fix; you know more about this place than I do, take my pig and leave me your goose." — "I shall risk something at that game," answered the lad, "but I will not be the cause of your getting into trouble." So he took the cord in his hand, and drove away the pig quickly along a by-path.

The good Hans, free from care, went homewards with the goose under his arm. "When I think over it properly," said he to himself, "I have even gained by the exchange; first there is the good roast-meat, then the quantity of fat which will drip from it, and which will give me dripping for my bread for a quarter of a year, and lastly the beautiful white feathers; I will have my pillow stuffed with them, and then indeed I shall go to sleep without rocking. How glad my mother will be!"

As he was going through the last village, there stood a scissors-grinder with his barrow; as his wheel whirred he sang — "I sharpen scissors and quickly grind, my coat blows out in the wind behind."

Hans stood still and looked at him; at last he spoke to him and said: "All's well with you, as you are so merry with your grinding." — "Yes," answered the scissors-grinder, "the trade has a golden foundation. A real grinder is a man who as often as he puts his hand into his pocket finds gold in it. But where did you buy that fine goose?"

"I did not buy it, but exchanged my pig for it." — "And the pig?" — "That I got for a cow." — "And the cow?" — "I took that instead of a horse." — "And the horse?" — "For that I gave a lump of gold as big as my head." — "And the gold?" — "Well, that was my wages for seven years' service." — "You have known how to look after yourself each time," said the grinder. "If you can only get on so far as to hear the money jingle in your pocket whenever you stand up, you will have made your fortune." "How shall I manage that?" said Hans. "You must be a grinder, as I am; nothing par-

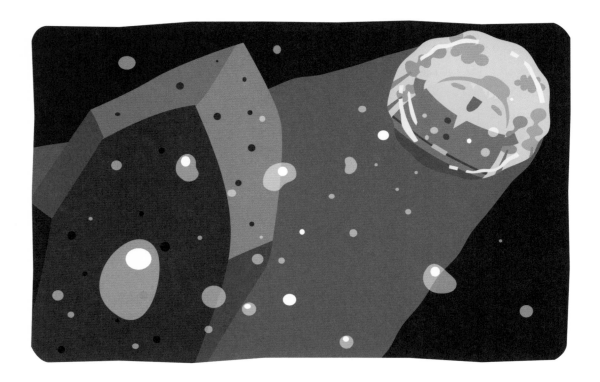

ticular is wanted for it but a grindstone, the rest finds itself. I have one here; it is certainly a little worn, but you need not give me anything for it but your goose; will you do it?"

"How can you ask?" answered Hans. "I shall be the luckiest fellow on earth; if I have money whenever I put my hand in my pocket, what need I trouble about any longer?" and he handed him the goose and received the grindstone in exchange. "Now," said the grinder, as he took up an ordinary heavy stone that lay by him, "here is a strong stone for you into the bargain; you can hammer well upon it, and straighten your old nails. Take it with you and keep it carefully."

Hans loaded himself with the stones, and went on with a contented heart; his eyes shone with joy. "I must have been born with a caul," he cried; "everything I want happens to me just as if I were a Sunday-child."

Meanwhile, as he had been on his legs since daybreak, he began to feel tired. Hunger also tormented him, for in his joy at the bargain by which he got the cow he had eaten up all his store of food at once. At last he could only go on with great trouble, and was forced to stop every minute; the stones, too, weighed him down dreadfully. Then he could not help thinking how nice it would be if he had not to carry them just then. He crept like a snail to a well in a field, and there he thought that he would rest and refresh himself with a cool draught of water, but in order that he might not injure the stones in sitting down, he laid them carefully by his side on the edge of the well. Then he sat down on it, and was to stoop and drink, when he made a slip, pushed against the stones, and both of them fell into the water. When Hans saw them with his own eyes sinking to the bottom, he jumped for joy, and then knelt down, and with tears in his eyes thanked God for having shown him this favour also, and delivered him in so good a way, and without his having any need to reproach himself, from those heavy stones which had been the only things that troubled him.

"There is no man under the sun so fortunate as I," he cried out. With a light heart and free from every burden he now ran on until he was with his mother at home.

Snow-White & Rose-Red

Illustrated by Margit Fellerer

There was once a poor widow who lived in a lonely cottage. In front of the cottage was a garden wherein stood two rose-trees, one of which bore white and the other red roses. She had two children who were like the two rose-trees, and one was called Snow-White, and the other Rose-Red. They were as good and happy, as busy and cheerful as ever two children in the world were, only Snow-White was more quiet and gentle than Rose-Red. Rose-Red liked better to run about in the meadows and fields seeking flowers and catching butterflies; but Snow-White sat at home with her mother, and helped her with her house-work, or read to her when there was nothing to do.

The two children were so fond of each another that they always held each other by the hand when they went out together, and when Snow-White said: "We will not leave each other," Rose-Red answered, "Never so long as we live," and their mother would add, "What one has she must share with the other."

They often ran about the forest alone and gathered red berries, and no beasts did them any harm, but came close to them trustfully. The little hare would eat a cabbage-leaf out of their hands, the roe grazed by their side, the stag leapt merrily by them, and the birds sat still upon the boughs, and sang whatever they knew.

No mishap overtook them; if they had stayed too late in the forest, and night came on, they laid themselves down near one another upon the moss, and slept until morning came, and their mother knew this and had no distress on their account. Once when they had spent the night in the wood and the dawn had roused them, they saw a beautiful child in a shining white dress sitting near their bed. He got up and looked quite kindly at them, but said nothing and went away into the forest. And when they looked round they found that they had been sleeping quite close to a precipice, and would certainly have fallen into it in the darkness if they had gone only a few paces further. And their mother told them that it must have been the angel who watches over good children.

Snow-White and Rose-Red kept their mother's little cottage so neat that it was a pleasure to look inside it. In the summer Rose-Red took care of the house, and every morning laid a wreath of flowers by her mother's bed before she awoke, in which was a rose from each tree. In the winter Snow-White lit the fire and hung the kettle on the wrekin. The kettle was of copper and shone like gold, so brightly was it polished. In the evening, when the snowflakes fell, the mother said: "Go, Snow-White, and bolt the door," and then they sat round the hearth, and the mother took her spectacles and read aloud out of a large book, and the two girls listened as they sat and span. And close by them lay a lamb upon the floor, and behind them upon a perch sat a white dove with its head hidden beneath its wings.

One evening, as they were thus sitting comfortably together, some one knocked at the door as if he wished to be let in. The mother said: "Quick, Rose-Red, open the door, it must be a traveller who is seeking shelter." Rose-Red went and pushed back the bolt, thinking that it was a poor man, but it was not; it was a bear that stretched his broad, black head within the door.

Rose-Red screamed and sprang back, the lamb bleated, the dove fluttered, and Snow-White hid herself behind her mother's bed. But the bear began to speak and said: "Do not be afraid, I will do you no harm! I am half-frozen, and only want to warm myself a little beside you."

"Poor bear," said the mother, "lie down by the fire, only take care that you do not burn your coat." Then she cried: "Snow-White, Rose-Red, come out, the bear will do you no harm, he means well." So they both came out, and by-and-by the lamb and dove came nearer, and were not afraid of him. The bear said: "Here, children, knock the snow out of my coat a little;" so they brought the broom and swept the bear's hide clean; and he stretched himself by the fire and growled contentedly and comfortably. It was not long before they grew quite at home, and played tricks with their clumsy guest. They tugged his hair with their hands, put their feet upon his back and rolled him about, or they took a hazel-switch and beat him, and when he growled they laughed. But the bear took it all in good part, only when they were too rough he called out:

"Leave me alive, children,
Snowy-White, Rosy-Red,
will you beat your lover dead?"

When it was bed-time, and the others went to bed, the mother said to the bear: "You can lie there by the hearth, and then you will be safe from the cold and the bad weather." As soon as day dawned the two children let him out, and he trotted across the snow into the forest.

Henceforth the bear came every evening at the same time, laid himself down by the hearth, and let the children amuse themselves with him as much as they liked; and they got so used to him that the doors were never fastened until their black friend had arrived.

When spring had come and all outside was green, the bear said one morning to Snow-White: "Now I must go away, and cannot come back for the whole summer." "Where are you going, then, dear bear?" asked Snow-White. "I must go into the forest and guard my treasures from the wicked dwarfs. In the winter, when the earth is frozen hard, they are obliged to stay below and cannot work their way through; but now, when the sun has thawed and warmed the earth, they break through it, and come out to pry and steal; and what once gets into their hands, and in their caves, does not easily see daylight again."

Snow-White was quite sorry for his going away, and as she unbolted the door for him, and the bear was hurrying out, he caught against the bolt and a piece of his hairy coat was torn off, and it seemed to Snow-White as if she had seen gold shining through it, but she was not sure about it. The bear ran away quickly, and was soon out of sight behind the trees.

A short time afterwards the mother sent her children into the forest to get firewood. There they found a big tree which lay felled on the ground, and close by the trunk something was jumping backwards and forwards in the grass, but they could not make out what it was. When they came nearer they saw a dwarf with an old withered face and a snow-white beard a yard long. The end of the beard

was caught in a crevice of the tree, and the little fellow was jumping backwards and forwards like a dog tied to a rope, and did not know what to do.

He glared at the girls with his fiery red eyes and cried: "Why do you stand there? Can you not come here and help me?" — "What are you about there, little man?" asked Rose-Red. "You stupid, prying goose!" answered the dwarf; "I was going to split the tree to get a little wood for cooking. The little bit of food that one of us wants gets burnt up directly with thick logs; we do not swallow so much as you coarse, greedy folk. I had just driven the wedge safely in, and everything was going as I wished; but the wretched wood was too smooth and suddenly sprang asunder, and the tree closed so quickly that I could not pull out my beautiful white beard; so now it is tight in and I cannot get away, and the silly, sleek, milk-faced things laugh! Ugh! how odious you are!" The children tried very hard, but they could not pull the beard out, it was caught too fast. "I will run and fetch some one," said Rose-Red. "You senseless goose!" snarled the dwarf; why should you fetch some one? You are already two too many for me; can you not think of something better?" — "Don't be impatient," said Snow-White, "I will help you," and she pulled her scissors out of her pocket, and cut off the end of the beard.

As soon as the dwarf felt himself free he laid hold of a bag which lay amongst the roots of the tree, and which was full of gold, and lifted it up, grumbling to himself: "Uncouth people, to cut off a piece of my fine beard. Bad luck to you!" and then he swung the bag upon his back, and went off without even once looking at the children.

Some time after that Snow-White and Rose-Red went to catch a dish of fish. As they came near the brook they saw something like a large grasshopper jumping towards the water, as if it were going to leap in. They ran to it and found it was the dwarf. "Where are you going?" said Rose-Red; "you surely don't want to go into the water?" — "I am not such a fool!" cried the dwarf; don't you see that the accursed fish wants to pull me in?" The little man had been sitting there fishing, and unluckily the wind had twisted his beard with the fishing-line; just then a big fish bit, and the feeble creature had not strength to pull it out; the fish kept the upper hand and pulled the dwarf towards him. He held on to all the reeds and rushes, but it was of little good, he was forced to follow the movements of the fish, and was in urgent danger of being dragged into the water.

The girls came just in time; they held him fast and tried to free his beard from the line, but all in vain, beard and line were entangled fast together. Nothing was left but to bring out the scissors and cut the beard, whereby a small part of it was lost. When the dwarf saw that he screamed out: "Is that civil, you toad-stool, to disfigure one's face? Was it not enough to clip off the end of my beard? Now you have cut off the best part of it. I cannot let myself be seen by my people. I wish you had been made to run the soles off your shoes!" Then he took out a sack of pearls which lay in the rushes, and without saying a word more he dragged it away and disappeared behind a stone.

It happened that soon afterwards the mother sent the two children to the town to buy needles and thread, and laces and ribbons. The road led them across a heath upon which huge pieces of rock lay strewn here and there. Now they noticed a large bird hovering in the air, flying slowly round and round above them; it sank lower and lower, and at last settled near a rock not far off. Directly afterwards they heard a loud, piteous cry. They ran up and saw with horror that the eagle had seized their old acquaintance the dwarf, and was going to carry him off.

The children, full of pity, at once took tight hold of the little man, and pulled against the eagle so long that at last he let his booty go. As soon as the dwarf had recovered from his first fright he cried with his shrill voice: "Could you not have done it more carefully! You dragged at my brown coat so that it is all torn and full of holes, you helpless clumsy creatures!" Then he took up a sack full of precious stones, and slipped away again under the rock into his hole. The girls, who by this time were used to his thanklessness, went on their way and did their business in the town.

As they crossed the heath again on their way home they surprised the dwarf, who had emptied out his bag of precious stones in a clean spot, and had not thought that anyone would come there so late. The evening sun shone upon the brilliant stones; they glittered and sparkled with all colors so beautifully that the children stood still and looked at them. "Why do you stand gaping there?" cried the dwarf, and his ashen-gray face became copper-red with rage. He was going on with his bad words when a loud growling was heard, and a black bear came trotting towards them out of the forest. The dwarf sprang up in a fright, but he could not get to his cave, for the bear was already close. Then in the dread of his heart he cried: "Dear Mr. Bear, spare me, I will give you all my treasures; look, the beautiful jewels lying there! Grant me my life; what do you want with such a slender little fellow as I? you would not feel me between your teeth. Come, take these two wicked girls, they are tender morsels for you, fat as young quails; for mercy's sake eat them!" The bear took no heed of his words, but gave the wicked creature a single blow with his paw, and he did not move again.

The girls had run away, but the bear called to them: "Snow-White and Rose-Red, do not be afraid; wait, I will come with you." Then they knew his voice and waited, and when he came up to them suddenly his bearskin fell off, and he stood there, a handsome man, clothed all in gold. "I am a King's son," he said, "and I was bewitched by that wicked dwarf, who had stolen my treasures; I have had to run about the forest as a savage bear until I was freed by his death. Now he has got his well-deserved punishment."

Snow-White was married to him, and Rose-Red to his brother, and they divided between them the great treasure which the dwarf had gathered together in his cave. The old mother lived peacefully and happily with her children for many years. She took the two rose-trees with her, and they stood before her window, and every year bore the most beautiful roses, white and red.

The Star-Money

Illustrated by Deanne Cheuk

There was once on a time a little girl whose father and mother were dead, and she was so poor that she no longer had any little room to live in, or bed to sleep in, and at last she had nothing else but the clothes she was wearing and a little bit of bread in her hand which some charitable soul had given her. She was, however, good and pious. And as she was thus forsaken by all the world, she went forth into the open country, trusting in the good God. Then a poor man met her, who said: "Ah, give me something to eat, I am so hungry!" She reached him the whole of her piece of bread, and said: "May God bless it to thy use," and went onwards. Then came a child who moaned and said: "My head is so cold, give me something to cover it with." So she took off her hood and gave it to him; and when she had walked a little farther, she met another child who had no jacket and was frozen with cold. Then she gave it her own; and a little farther on one begged for a frock, and she gave away that also. At length she got into a forest and it had already become dark, and there came yet another child, and asked for a little shirt, and the good little girl thought to herself: "It is a dark night and no one sees thee, thou canst very well give thy little shirt away," and took it off, and gave away that also. And as she so stood, and had not one single thing left, suddenly some stars from heaven fell down, and they were nothing else but hard smooth pieces of money, and although she had just given her little shirt away, she had a new one which was of the very finest linen. Then she gathered together the money into this, and was rich all the days of her life.

Mother Holle

Illustrated by A-Linha

There was once a widow who had two daughters – one of whom was pretty and industrious, whilst the other was ugly and idle. But she was much fonder of the ugly and idle one, because she was her own daughter; and the other, who was a step-daughter, was obliged to do all the work, and be the Cinderella of the house. Every day the poor girl had to sit by a well, in the highway, and spin and spin till her fingers bled.

Now it happened that one day the shuttle was marked with her blood, so she dipped it in the well, to wash the mark off; but it dropped out of her hand and fell to the bottom. She began to weep, and ran to her step-mother and told her of the mishap. But she scolded her sharply, and was so merciless as to say: "Since you have let the shuttle fall in, you must fetch it out again."

So the girl went back to the well, and did not know what to do; and in the sorrow of her heart she jumped into the well to get the shuttle. She lost her senses; and when she awoke and came to herself again, she was in a lovely meadow where the sun was shining and many thousands of flowers were growing. Along this meadow she went, and at last came to a baker's oven full of bread, and the bread cried out: "Oh, take me out! take me out! or I shall burn; I have been baked a long time!" So she went up to it, and took out all the loaves one after another with the bread-shovel. After that she went on till she came to a tree covered with apples, which called out to her: "Oh, shake me! shake me! we apples are all ripe!" So she shook the tree till the apples fell like rain, and went on shaking till they were all down, and when she had gathered them into a heap, she went on her way.

At last she came to a little house, out of which an old woman peeped; but she had such large teeth that the girl was frightened, and was about to run away.

But the old woman called out to her: "What are you afraid of, dear child? Stay with me; if you will do all the work in the house properly, you shall be the better for it. Only you must take care to make my bed well, and shake it thoroughly till the feathers fly – for then there is snow on the earth. I am Mother Holle."

As the old woman spoke so kindly to her, the girl took courage and agreed to enter her service. She attended to everything to the satisfaction of her mistress, and always shook her bed so vigorously that the feathers flew about like snow-flakes. So she had a pleasant life with her; never an angry word; and boiled or roast meat every day.

She stayed some time with Mother Holle, and then she became sad. At first she did not know what was the matter with her, but found at length that it was home-sickness: although she was many thousand times better off here than at home, still she had a longing to be there. At last she said to the old woman: "I have a longing for home; and however well off I am down here, I cannot stay any longer; I must go up again to my own people." Mother Holle said: "I am pleased that you long for your home again, and as you have served me so truly, I myself will take you up again."

Thereupon she took her by the hand, and led her to a large door. The door was opened, and just as the maiden was standing beneath the doorway, a heavy shower of golden rain fell, and all the gold remained sticking to her, so that she was completely covered over with it.

"You shall have that because you have been so industrious," said Mother Holle, and at the same time she gave her back the shuttle which she had let fall into the well. Thereupon the door closed, and the maiden found herself up above upon the earth, not far from her mother's house. And as she went into the yard the cock was standing by the well-side, and cried:

"Cock-a-doodle-doo! Your golden girl's come back to you!"

So she went in to her mother, and as she arrived thus covered with gold, she was well received, both by her and her sister. The girl told all that had happened to her; and as soon as the mother heard how she had come by so much wealth, she was very anxious to obtain the same good luck for the ugly and lazy daughter. She had to seat herself by the well and spin; and in order that her shuttle might be stained

with blood, she stuck her hand into a thorn bush and pricked her finger. Then she threw her shuttle into the well, and jumped in after it.

She came, like the other, to the beautiful meadow and walked along the very same path. When she got to the oven the bread again cried: "Oh, take me out! take me out! or I shall burn; I have been baked a long time!" But the lazy thing answered: "As if I had any wish to make myself dirty?" and on she went. Soon she came to the apple-tree, which cried: "Oh, shake me! shake me! we apples are all ripe!" But she answered: "I like that! one of you might fall on my head," and so went on. When she came to Mother Holle's house she was not afraid, for she had already heard of her big teeth, and she hired herself to her immediately.

The first day she forced herself to work diligently, and obeyed Mother Holle when she told her to do anything, for she was thinking of all the gold that she would give her. But on the second day she began to be lazy, and on the third day still more so, and then she would not get up in the morning at all. Neither did she make Mother Holle's bed as she ought, and did not shake it so as to make the feathers fly up. Mother Holle was soon tired of this, and gave her notice to leave. The lazy girl was willing enough to go, and thought that now the golden rain would come. Mother Holle led her also to the great door; but while she was standing beneath it, instead of the gold a big kettleful of pitch was emptied over her. "That is the reward for your service," said Mother Holle, and shut the door. So the lazy girl went home; but she was quite covered with pitch, and the cock by the well-side, as soon as he saw her, cried out:

"Cock-a-doodle-doo! Your pitchy girl's come back to you!"

But the pitch stuck fast to her, and could not be got off as long as she lived.

The Wolf
and the Seven Little Kids

Illustrated by Judith Drews & Hans Baltzer

There was once upon a time an old goat who had seven little kids, and loved them with all the love of a mother for her children. One day she wanted to go into the forest and fetch some food. So she called all seven to her and said: "Dear children, I have to go into the forest, be on your guard against the wolf; if he come in, he will devour you all – skin, hair, and all. The wretch often disguises himself, but you will know him at once by his rough voice and his black feet." The kids said: "Dear mother, we will take good care of ourselves; you may go away without any anxiety." Then the old one bleated, and went on her way with an easy mind.

It was not long before some one knocked at the house-door and called: "Open the door, dear children; your mother is here, and has brought something back with her for each of you." But the little kids knew that it was the wolf, by the rough voice; "We will not open the door," cried they, "thou art not our mother. She has a soft, pleasant voice, but thy voice is rough; thou art the wolf!" Then the wolf went away to a shopkeeper and bought himself a great lump of chalk, ate this and made his voice soft with it. The he came back, knocked at the door of the house, and cried: "Open the door, dear children, your mother is here and has brought something back with her for each of you." But the wolf had laid his black paws against the window, and the children saw them and cried: "We will not open the door, our mother has not black feet like thee; thou art the wolf." Then the wolf ran to a baker and said: "I have hurt my feet, rub some dough over them for me." And when the baker had rubbed his feet over, he ran to the miller and said: "Strew some white meal over my feet for me." The miller thought to himself: "The wolf wants to deceive someone," and refused; but the wolf said, "If thou wilt not do it, I will devour thee." Then the miller was afraid, and made his paws white for him. Truly men are like that.

So now the wretch went for the third time to the house-door, knocked at it and said: "Open the door for me, children, your dear little mother has come home, and has brought every one of you something back from the forest with her." The little kids cried: "First show us thy paws that we may know if thou art our dear little mother." Then he put his paws in through the window, and when the kids saw that they were white, they believed that all he said was true, and opened the door. But who should come in but the wolf! They were terrified and wanted to hide themselves. One sprang under the table, the second into the bed, the third into the stove, the fourth into the kitchen, the fifth into the cupboard, the sixth under the washing-bowl, and the seventh into the clock-case. But the wolf found them all, and used no great ceremony; one after the other he swallowed them down his throat. The youngest, who was in the clock-case, was the only one he did not find. When the wolf had satisfied his appetite he took himself off, laid himself down under a tree in the green meadow outside, and began to sleep. Soon afterwards the old goat came home again from the forest. Ah! What a sight she saw there! The house-door stood wide open. The table, chairs, and benches were thrown down, the washing-bowl lay broken to pieces, and the quilts and pillows were pulled off the bed. She sought her children, but they were nowhere to be found. She called them one after another by name, but no one answered. At last, when she came to the youngest, a soft voice cried: "Dear mother, I am in the clock-case." She took the kid out, and it told her that the wolf had come and had eaten all the others. Then you may imagine how she wept over her poor children.

At length in her grief she went out, and the youngest kid ran with her. When they came to the meadow, there lay the wolf by the tree and snored so loud that the branches shook. She looked at him on every side and saw that something was moving and struggling in his gorged belly. "Ah, heavens," said she, "is it possible that my poor children whom he has swallowed down for his supper, can be still alive?" Then the kid had to run home and fetch scissors, and a needle and thread, and the goat cut open the monster's stomach, and hardly had she make one cut,

READYMIX

than one little kid thrust its head out, and when she cut farther, all six sprang out one after another, and were all still alive, and had suffered no injury whatever, for in his greediness the monster had swallowed them down whole. What rejoicing there was! They embraced their dear mother, and jumped like a sailor at his wedding. The mother, however, said: "Now go and look for some big stones, and we will fill the wicked beast's stomach with them while he is still asleep." Then the seven kids dragged the stones thither with all speed, and put as many of them into his stomach as they could get in; and the mother sewed him up again in the greatest haste, so that he was not aware of anything and never once stirred.

When the wolf at length had had his sleep out, he got on his legs, and as the stones in his stomach made him very thirsty, he wanted to go to a well to drink. But when he began to walk and move about, the stones in his stomach knocked against each other and rattled. Then cried he:

"What rumbles and tumbles
Against my poor bones?
I thought 'twas six kids,
But it's naught but big stones."

And when he got to the well and stooped over the water and was just about to drink, the heavy stones made him fall in, and there was no help, but he had to drown miserably. When the seven kids saw that, they came running to the spot and cried aloud: "The wolf is dead! The wolf is dead!" and danced for joy round about the well with their mother.

The Valiant Little Tailor

Illustrated by Annlaug Auestad

One summer's morning a little tailor was sitting on his table by the window; he was in good spirits, and sewed with all his might. Then came a peasant woman down the street crying: "Good jams, cheap! Good jams, cheap!" This rang pleasantly in the tailor's ears; he stretched his delicate head out of the window, and called: "Come up here, dear woman; here you will get rid of your goods." The woman came up the three steps to the tailor with her heavy basket, and he made her unpack the whole of the pots for him. He inspected all of them, lifted them up, put his nose to them, and at length said: "The jam seems to me to be good, so weigh me out four ounces, dear woman, and if it is a quarter of a pound that is of no consequence." The woman who had hoped to find a good sale, gave him what he desired, but went away quite angry and grumbling. "Now, God bless the jam to my use," cried the little tailor, "and give me health and strength;" so he brought the bread out of the cupboard, cut himself a piece right across the loaf and spread the jam over it. "This won't taste bitter," said he, "but I will just finish the jacket before I take a bite." He laid the bread near him, sewed on, and in his joy, made bigger and bigger stitches. In the meantime the smell of the sweet jam ascended so to the wall, where the flies were sitting in great numbers, that they were attracted and descended on it in hosts. "Hola! who invited you?" said the little tailor, and drove the unbidden guests away. The flies, however, who understood no German, would not be turned away, but came back again in ever-increasing companies. The little tailor at last lost all patience, and got a bit of cloth from the hole under his work-table, and saying: "Wait, and I will give it to you," struck it mercilessly on them. When he drew it away and counted, there lay before him no fewer than seven, dead and with legs stretched out. "Art thou a fellow of that sort?" said he, and could not help admiring his own bravery. "The whole town shall know of this!" And the little tailor hastened to cut himself a girdle, stitched it, and embroidered on it in large letters: "Seven at one stroke!" — "What, the town!" he continued, "The whole world shall hear of it!" and his heart wagged with joy like a lamb's tail. The tailor put on the girdle, and resolved to go forth into the world, because he thought his workshop was too small for his valour. Before he went away, he sought about in the house to see if there was anything which he could take with him; however, he found nothing but an old cheese, and that he put in his pocket. In front of the door he observed a bird which had caught itself in the thicket. It had to go into his pocket with the cheese.

Now he took to the road boldly, and as he was light and nimble, he felt no fatigue. The road led him up a mountain, and when he had reached the highest point of it, there sat a powerful giant looking about him quite comfortably. The little tailor went bravely up, spoke to him, and said: "Good day, comrade, so thou art sitting there overlooking the wide-spread world! I am just on my way thither, and want to try my luck. Hast thou any inclination to go with me?" The giant looked contemptuously at the tailor, and said: "Thou ragamuffin! Thou miserable creature!"

"Oh, indeed?" answered the little tailor, and unbuttoned his coat, and showed the giant the girdle, "There mayst thou read what kind of a man I am!" The giant read: "Seven at one stroke," and thought that they had been men whom the tailor had killed, and began to feel a little respect for the tiny fellow. Nevertheless, he wished to try him first, and took a stone in his hand and squeezed it together so that water dropped out of it. "Do that likewise," said the giant, "if thou hast strength?" — "Is that all?" said the tailor, "that is child's play with us!" and put his hand into his pocket, brought out the soft cheese, and pressed it until the liquid ran out of it. "Faith," said he, "that was a little better, wasn't it?" The giant did not know what to say, and could not believe it of the little man. Then the giant picked up a stone and threw it so high that the eye could scarcely follow it. "Now, little mite of a man, do that likewise." — "Well thrown," said the tailor, "but after all the stone came down to earth again; I will throw you one which shall never come back at all." And he put his hand into his pocket, took out the bird, and threw it into the air. The bird, delighted with its liberty, rose, flew away and did not come back. "How does that shot please you, comrade?" asked the tailor. "Thou canst certainly throw," said the giant, "but now we will see if thou art able to carry any-thing properly." He took the little tailor to a mighty oak tree which lay there felled on the ground, and said: "If thou art strong enough, help me to carry the tree out of the forest." — "Readily," answered the little man; "take thou the trunk on thy shoulders, and I will raise up the branches and twigs; after all, they are the heaviest." The giant took the trunk on his shoulder, but the tailor seated himself on a branch, and the giant who could not look round, had to carry away the whole tree, and the little tailor into the bargain: he behind, was quite merry and happy, and whistled the song: "Three tailors rode forth from the gate," as if carrying the tree were child's play. The giant, after he had dragged the heavy burden part of the way, could go no further, and cried: "Hark you, I shall have to let the tree fall!" The tailor sprang nimbly down, seized the tree with both arms as if he had been carrying it, and said to the giant: "Thou art such a great fellow, and yet canst not even carry the tree!"

They went on together, and as they passed a cherry-tree, the giant laid hold of the top of the tree where the ripest fruit was hanging, bent it down, gave it into the tailor's hand, and bade him eat. But the little tailor was much too weak to hold the tree, and when the giant let it go, it sprang back again, and the tailor was hurried into the air with it. When he had fallen down again without injury, the giant said: "What is this? Hast thou not strength enough to hold the weak twig?" "There is no lack of strength," answered the little tailor. "Dost thou think that could be anything to a man who has struck down seven at one blow? I leapt over the tree because the huntsmen are shooting down there in the thicket. Jump as I did, if thou canst do it." The giant made the attempt, but could not get over the tree, and remained hanging in the branches, so that in this also the tailor kept the upper hand.

The giant said: "If thou art such a valiant fellow, come with me into our cavern and spend the night with us." The little tailor was willing, and followed him. When they went into the cave, other giants were sitting there by the fire, and each of them had a roasted sheep in his hand and was eating it. The little tailor looked round and thought: "It is much more spacious here than in my workshop." The giant showed him a bed, and said he was to lie down in it and sleep. The bed, however, was too big for the little tailor; he did not lie down in it, but crept into a corner.

83

When it was midnight, and the giant thought that the little tailor was lying in a sound sleep, he got up, took a great iron bar, cut through the bed with one blow, and thought he had given the grasshopper his finishing stroke. With the earliest dawn the giants went into the forest, and had quite forgotten the little tailor, when all at once he walked up to them quite merrily and boldly. The giants were terrified, they were afraid that he would strike them all dead, and ran away in a great hurry. The little tailor went onwards, always following his own pointed nose. After he had walked for a long time, he came to the courtyard of a royal palace, and as he felt weary, he lay down on the grass and fell asleep. Whilst he lay there, the people came and inspected him on all sides, and read on his girdle: "Seven at one stroke." "Ah," said they, "What does the great warrior here in the midst of peace? He must be a mighty lord." They went and announced him to the King, and gave it as their opinion that if war should break out, this would be a weighty and useful man who ought on no account to be allowed to depart. The counsel pleased the King, and he sent one of his courtiers to the little tailor to offer him military service when he awoke. The ambassador remained standing by the sleeper, waited until he stretched his limbs and opened his eyes, and then conveyed to him this proposal. "For this very reason have I come here," the tailor replied, "I am ready to enter the King's service." He was therefore honorably received and a special dwelling was assigned him.

The soldiers, however, were set against the little tailor, and wished him a thousand miles away. "What is to be the end of this?" they said amongst themselves. "If we quarrel with him, and he strikes about him, seven of us will fall at every blow; not one of us can stand against him." They came therefore to a decision, betook themselves in a body to the King, and begged for their dismissal. "We are not prepared," said they, "to stay with a man who kills seven at one stroke." The King was sorry that for the sake of one he should lose all his faithful servants, wished that he had never set eyes on the tailor, and would willingly have been rid of him again. But he did not venture to give him his dismissal, for he dreaded lest he should strike him and all his people dead, and place himself on the royal throne. He thought about it for a long time, and at last found good counsel. He sent to the little tailor and caused him to be informed that as he was such a great warrior, he had one request to make to him. In a forest of his country lived two giants who caused great mischief with their robbing, murdering, ravaging, and burning, and no one could approach them without putting himself in danger of death. If the tailor conquered and killed these two giants, he would give him his only daughter to wife, and half of his kingdom as a dowry, likewise one hundred horsemen should go with him to assist him. "That would indeed be a fine thing for a man like me!" thought the little tailor. "One is not offered a beautiful princess and half a kingdom every day of one's life!" — "Oh, yes," he replied, "I will soon subdue the giants, and do not require the help of the hundred horsemen to do it; he who can hit seven with one blow has no need to be afraid of two."

The little tailor went forth, and the hundred horsemen followed him. When he came to the outskirts of the forest, he said to his followers: "Just stay waiting here, I alone will soon finish off the giants." Then he bounded into the forest and looked about right and left. After a while he perceived both giants. They lay sleeping under a tree, and snored so that the branches waved up and down. The little tailor, not idle, gathered two pocketsful of stones, and with these climbed up the tree. When he was half-way up, he slipped down by a branch, until he sat just above

the sleepers, and then let one stone after another fall on the breast of one of the giants. For a long time the giant felt nothing, but at last he awoke, pushed his comrade, and said: "Why art thou knocking me?" — "Thou must be dreaming," said the other, "I am not knocking thee." They laid themselves down to sleep again, and then the tailor threw a stone down on the second. "What is the meaning of this?" cried the other. "Why art thou pelting me?" — "I am not pelting thee," answered the first, growling. They disputed about it for a time, but as they were weary they let the matter rest, and their eyes closed once more. The little tailor began his game again, picked out the biggest stone, and threw it with all his might on the breast of the first giant. "That is too bad!" cried he, and sprang up like a madman, and pushed his companion against the tree until it shook. The other paid him back in the same coin, and they got into such a rage that they tore up trees and belabored each other so long, that at last they both fell down dead on the ground at the same time. Then the little tailor leapt down. "It is a lucky thing," said he, "that they did not tear up the tree on which I was sitting, or I should have had to spring on to another like a squirrel; but we tailors are nimble." He drew out his sword and gave each of them a couple of thrusts in the breast, and then went out to the horsemen and said: "The work is done; I have given both of them their finishing stroke, but it was hard work! They tore up trees in their sore need, and defended themselves with them, but all that is to no purpose when a man like myself comes, who can kill seven at one blow." — "But are you not wounded?" asked the horsemen. "You need not concern yourself about that," answered the tailor, "They have not bent one hair of mine." The horsemen would not believe him, and rode into the forest; there they found the giants swimming in their blood, and all round about lay the torn-up trees.

The little tailor demanded of the King the promised reward; he, however, repented of his promise, and again bethought himself how he could get rid of the hero. "Before thou receivest my daughter, and the half of my kingdom," said he to him, "thou must perform one more heroic deed. In the forest roams a unicorn which does great harm, and thou must catch it first." — "I fear one unicorn still less than two giants. Seven at one blow, is my kind of affair." He took a rope and an axe with him, went forth into the forest, and again bade those who were sent with him to wait outside. He had not to seek long. The unicorn soon came towards him, and rushed directly on the tailor, as if it would spit him on his horn without more ceremony. "Softly, softly; it can't be done as quickly as that," said he, and stood still and waited until the animal was quite close, and then sprang nimbly behind the tree. The unicorn ran against the tree with all its strength, and struck its horn so fast in the trunk that it had not strength enough to draw it out again, and thus it was caught. "Now, I have got the bird," said the tailor, and came out from behind the tree and put the rope round its neck, and then with his axe he hewed the horn out of the tree, and when all was ready he led the beast away and took it to the King.

The King still would not give him the promised reward, and made a third demand. Before the wedding the tailor was to catch him a wild boar that made great havoc in the forest, and the huntsmen should give him their help. "Willingly," said the tailor, "that is child's play!" He did not take the huntsmen with him into the forest, and they were well pleased that he did not, for the wild boar had several times received them in such a manner that they had no inclination to lie in wait for him. When the boar perceived the tailor, it ran on him with foaming mouth and whetted tusks, and was about to throw him to the ground, but the active hero sprang into a chapel which was near, and up to the window at once, and in one bound out again. The boar ran in after him, but the tailor ran round outside and shut the door behind it, and then the raging beast, which was much too heavy and awkward to leap out of the window, was caught. The little tailor called the huntsmen thither that they might see the prisoner with their own eyes. The hero, however went to the King, who was now, whether he liked it or not, obliged to keep his promise, and gave him his daughter and the half of his kingdom. Had he known that it was no warlike hero, but a little tailor who was standing before him, it would have gone to his heart still more than it did. The wedding was held with great magnificence and small joy, and out of a tailor a king was made.

After some time the young Queen heard her husband say in his dreams at night: "Boy, make me the doublet, and patch the pantaloons, or else I will rap the yard-measure over thine ears." Then she discovered in what state of life the young lord had been born, and next morning complained of her wrongs to her father, and begged him to help her to get rid of her husband, who was nothing else but a tailor.

The King comforted her and said: "Leave thy bed-room door open this night, and my servants shall stand outside, and when he has fallen asleep shall go in, bind him, and take him on board a ship which shall carry him into the wide world." The woman was satisfied with this; but the King's armour-bearer, who had heard all, was friendly with the young lord, and informed him of the whole plot. "I'll put a screw into that business," said the little tailor. At night he went to bed with his wife at the usual time, and when she thought that he had fallen asleep, she got up, opened the door, and then lay down again. The little tailor, who was only pretending to be asleep, began to cry out in a clear voice: "Boy, make me the doublet and patch me the pantaloons, or I will rap the yard-measure over thine ears. I smote seven at one blow. I killed two giants, I brought away one unicorn and caught a wild boar, and am I to fear those who are standing outside the room." When these men heard the tailor speaking thus, they were overcome by a great dread, and ran as if the wild huntsman were behind them, and none of them would venture anything further against him. So the little tailor was a king and remained one, to the end of his life.

The Wishing-Table, Gold-Ass, and the Cudgel in the Sack

Illustrated by Dan Abbott

There was once upon a time a tailor who had three sons, and only one goat. But as the goat supported the whole of them with her milk, she was obliged to have good food, and to be taken every day to pasture. The sons, therefore, did this, in turn. Once the eldest took her to the churchyard, where the finest herbs were to be found, and let her eat and run about there. At night when it was time to go home he asked: "Goat, hast thou had enough?" The goat answered:

"I have eaten so much, not a leaf more I'll touch, meh! meh!"

"Come home, then," said the youth, and took hold of the cord round her neck, led her into the stable and tied her up securely. "Well," said the old tailor, "has the goat had as much food as she ought?" — "Oh," answered the son, "she has eaten so much, not a leaf more she'll touch." But the father wished to satisfy himself, and went down to the stable, stroked the dear animal and asked: "Goat, art thou satisfied?" The goat answered:

"Wherewithal should I be satisfied? Among the graves I leapt about,
And found no food, so went without, meh! meh!"

"What do I hear?" cried the tailor, and ran upstairs and said to the youth, "Hollo, thou liar: thou saidest the goat had had enough, and hast let her hunger!" and in his anger he took the yard-measure from the wall, and drove him out with blows.

Next day it was the turn of the second son, who looked out for a place in the fence of the garden, where nothing but good herbs grew, and the goat cleared them all off. At night when he wanted to go home, he asked: "Goat, art thou satisfied?" The goat answered:

"I have eaten so much, not a leaf more I'll touch, meh! meh!"

"Come home, then," said the youth, and led her home, and tied her up in the stable. "Well," said the old tailor, "has the goat had as much food as she ought?" "Oh," answered the son, "she has eaten so much, not a leaf more she'll touch." The tailor would not rely on this, but went down to the stable and said: "Goat, hast thou had enough?" The goat answered:

"Wherewithal should I be satisfied? Among the graves I leapt about,
And found no food, so went without, meh! meh!"

"The godless wretch!" cried the tailor, "to let such a good animal hunger," and he ran up and drove the youth out of doors with the yard-measure.
Now came the turn of the third son, who wanted to do the thing well, and sought out some bushes with the finest leaves, and let the goat devour them. In the evening when he wanted to go home, he asked: "Goat, hast thou had enough?" The goat answered:

"I have eaten so much, not a leaf more I'll touch, meh! meh!"

"Come home, then," said the youth, and led her into the stable, and tied her up. "Well," said the old tailor, "has the goat had a proper amount of food?" — "She has eaten so much, not a leaf more she'll touch." The tailor did not trust to that, but went down and asked: "Goat, hast thou had enough?" The wicked beast answered:

"Wherewithal should I be satisfied? Among the graves I leapt about,
And found no leaves, so went without, meh! meh!"

"Oh, the brood of liars!" cried the tailor, "each as wicked and forgetful of his duty as the other! Ye shall no longer make a fool of me," and quite beside himself with anger, he ran upstairs and belaboured the poor young fellow so vigorously with the yard-measure that he sprang out of the house.

The old tailor was now alone with his goat. Next morning he went down into the stable, caressed the goat and said: "Come, my dear little animal, I will take thee to feed myself." He took her by the rope and conducted her to green hedges, and amongst milfoil, and whatever else goats like to eat. "There thou mayest for once eat to thy heart's content," said he to her, and let her browse till evening. Then he asked: "Goat, art thou satisfied?" She replied:

"I have eaten so much, not a leaf more I'll touch, meh! meh!"

"Come home, then," said the tailor, and led her into the stable, and tied her fast. When he was going away, he turned round again and said: "Well, art thou satisfied for once?" But the goat did not behave the better to him, and cried:

"Wherewithal should I be satisfied? Among the graves I leapt about,
And found no leaves, so went without, meh! meh!"

When the tailor heard that, he was shocked, and saw clearly that he had driven away his three sons without cause. "Wait, thou ungrateful creature," cried he, "it is not enough to drive thee forth, I will mark thee so that thou wilt no more dare to show thyself amongst honest tailors." In great haste he ran upstairs, fetched his razor, lathered the goat's head, and shaved her as clean as the palm of his hand. And as the yard-measure would have been too good for her, he brought the horse-whip, and gave her such cuts with it that she ran away in violent haste.

When the tailor was thus left quite alone in his house he fell into great grief, and would gladly have had his sons back again, but no one knew whither they were gone. The eldest had apprenticed himself to a joiner, and learnt industriously and indefatigably, and when the time came for him to go travelling, his master presented him with a little table which had no particular appearance, and was made of common wood, but it had one good property; if anyone set it out, and said: "Little table, spread thyself," the good little table was at once covered with a clean little cloth, and a plate was there, and a knife and fork beside it, and dishes with boiled meats and roasted meats, as many as there was room for, and a great glass of red wine shone so that it made the heart glad. The young journeyman thought: "With this thou hast enough for thy whole life," and went joyously about the world and never troubled himself at all whether an inn was good or bad, or if anything was to be found in it or not. When it suited him he did not enter an inn at all, but either on the plain, in a wood, a meadow, or wherever he fancied, he took his little table off his back, set it down before him, and said: "Cover thyself," and then everything appeared that his heart desired. At length he took it into his head to go back to his father, whose anger would now be appeased, and who would now willingly receive him with his wishing-table.

It came to pass that on his way home, he came one evening to an inn which was filled with guests. They bade him welcome, and invited him to sit and eat with them, for otherwise he would have difficulty in getting anything. "No," answered the joiner, "I will not take the few bites out of your mouths; rather than that, you shall be my guests." They laughed, and thought he was jesting with them; he, however, placed his wooden table in the middle of the room, and said: "Little table, cover thyself." Instantly it was covered with food, so good that the host could never have procured it, and the smell of it ascended pleasantly to the nostrils of the guests. "Fall to, dear friends," said the joiner; and the guests when they saw that he meant it, did not need to be asked twice, but drew near, pulled out their knives and attacked it valiantly. And what surprised them the most was that when a dish became empty, a full one instantly took its place of its own accord. The innkeeper stood in one corner and watched the affair; he did not at all know what to say, but thought: "Thou couldst easily find a use for such a cook as that in thy kitchen." The joiner and his comrades made merry until late into the night; at length they lay down to sleep, and the young apprentice also went to bed, and set his magic table against the wall. The host's thoughts, however, let him have no rest; it occurred to him that there was a little old table in his lumber-room which looked just like the apprentice's and he brought it out quite softly, and exchanged it for the wishing-table. Next morning, the joiner paid for his bed, took up his table, never thinking that he had got a false one, and went his way. At mid-day he reached his father, who received him with great joy. "Well, my dear son, what hast thou learnt?" said he to him. "Father, I have become a joiner." "A good trade," replied the old man; "but what hast thou brought back with thee from thy apprenticeship?" — "Father, the best thing which I have brought back with me is this little table." The tailor inspected it on all sides and said: "Thou didst not make a masterpiece when thou mad'st that; it is a bad old table." — "But it is a table which furnishes itself," replied the son. "When I set it out, and tell it to cover itself, the most beautiful dishes stand on it, and a wine also, which gladdens the heart. Just invite all our relations and friends, they shall refresh and enjoy themselves for once, for the table will give them all they require." When the company was assembled, he put his table in the middle of the room and said: "Little table, cover thyself," but the little table did not bestir itself, and remained just as bare as any other table which did not understand language. Then the poor apprentice became aware that his table had been changed, and was ashamed at having to stand there like a liar. The relations, however, mocked him, and were forced to go home without having eaten or drunk. The father brought out his patches again, and went on tailoring, but the son went to a master in the craft.

The second son had gone to a miller and had apprenticed himself to him. When his years were over, the master said: "As thou hast conducted thyself so well, I give thee an ass of a peculiar kind, which neither draws a cart nor carries a sack." "To what use is he put, then?" asked the young apprentice. "He lets gold drop from his mouth," answered the miller. "If thou settest him on a cloth and sayest 'Bricklebrit,' the good animal will drop gold pieces for thee." — "That is a fine thing," said the apprentice, and thanked the master, and went out into the world. When he had need of gold, he had only to say "Bricklebrit" to his ass, and it rained gold pieces, and he had nothing to do but pick them off the ground. Wheresoever he went, the best of everything was good enough for him, and the dearer the better, for he had always a full purse. When he had looked about the world for some time, he thought: "Thou must seek out thy father; if thou goest to him with the gold-ass he will forget his anger, and receive thee well." It came to pass that he came to the same public-house in which his brother's table had been exchanged. He led his ass by the bridle, and the host was about to take the animal from him and tie him up, but the young apprentice said: "Don't trouble yourself,

I will take my grey horse into the stable, and tie him up myself too, for I must know where he stands." This struck the host as odd, and he thought that a man who was forced to look after his ass himself, could not have much to spend; but when the stranger put his hand in his pocket and brought out two gold pieces, and said he was to provide something good for him, the host opened his eyes wide, and ran and sought out the best he could muster. After dinner the guest asked what he owed. The host did not see why he should not double the reckoning, and said the apprentice must give two more gold pieces. He felt in his pocket, but his gold was just at an end. "Wait an instant, sir host," said he, "I will go and fetch some money;" but he took the table-cloth with him. The host could not imagine what this could mean, and being curious, stole after him, and as the guest bolted the stable-door, he peeped through a hole left by a knot in the wood. The stranger spread out the cloth under the animal and cried: "Bricklebrit," and immediately the beast began to let gold pieces fall, so that it fairly rained down money on the ground. "Eh, my word," said the host, "ducats are quickly coined there! A purse like that is not amiss." The guest paid his score, and went to bed, but in the night the host stole down into the stable, led away the master of the mint, and tied up another ass in his place.

Early next morning the apprentice travelled away with his ass, and thought that he had his gold-ass. At mid-day he reached his father, who rejoiced to see him again, and gladly took him in. "What hast thou made of thyself, my son?" asked the old man. "A miller," dear father, he answered. "What hast thou brought back with thee from thy travels?" — "Nothing else but an ass." — "There are asses enough here," said the father, "I would rather have had a good goat." — "Yes," replied the son, "but it is no common ass, but a gold-ass, when I say 'Bricklebrit,' the good beast opens its mouth and drops a whole sheetful of gold pieces. Just summon all our relations hither, and I will make them rich folks." — "That suits me well," said the tailor, "for then I shall have no need to torment myself any longer with the needle," and ran out himself and called the relations together. As soon as they were assembled, the miller bade them make way, spread out his cloth, and brought the ass into the room. "Now watch," said he, and cried, "Bricklebrit," but no gold pieces fell, and it was clear that the animal knew nothing of the art, for every ass does not attain such perfection. Then the poor miller pulled a long face,

saw that he was betrayed, and begged pardon of the relatives, who went home as poor as they came. There was no help for it, the old man had to betake him to his needle once more, and the youth hired himself to a miller.

The third brother had apprenticed himself to a turner, and as that is skilled labour, he was the longest in learning. His brothers, however, told him in a letter how badly things had gone with them, and how the innkeeper had cheated them of their beautiful wishing-gifts on the last evening before they reached home. When the turner had served his time, and had to set out on his travels, as he had conducted himself so well, his master presented him with a sack and said: "There is a cudgel in it." — "I can put on the sack," said he, "and it may be of good service to me, but why should the cudgel be in it? It only makes it heavy." — "I will tell thee why," replied the master; "if any one has done anything to injure thee, do but say, 'Out of the sack, Cudgel!' and the cudgel will leap forth among the people, and play such a dance on their backs that they will not be able to stir or move for a week, and it will not leave off until thou sayest, 'Into the sack, Cudgel!'" The apprentice thanked him, and put the sack on his back, and when any one came too near him, and wished to attack him, he said: "Out of the sack, Cudgel!'" and instantly the cudgel sprang out, and dusted the coat or jacket of one after the other on their backs, and never stopped until it had stripped it off them, and it was done so quickly, that before anyone was aware, it was already his own turn.

In the evening the young turner reached the inn where his brothers had been cheated. He laid his sack on the table before him, and began to talk of all the wonderful things which he had seen in the world. "Yes," said he, "people may easily find a table which will cover itself, a gold-ass, and things of that kind – extremely good things which I by no means despise – but these are nothing in comparison with the treasure which I have won for myself, and am carrying about with me in my sack there." The inn-keeper pricked up his ears: "What in the world can that be?" thought he; "the sack must be filled with nothing but jewels; I ought to get them cheap too, for all good things go in threes." When it was time for sleep, the guest stretched himself on the bench, and laid his sack beneath him for a pillow. When the inn-keeper thought his guest was lying in a sound sleep, he went to him and pushed and pulled quite gently and carefully at the sack to see if he could possibly draw it away and lay another in its place. The turner had, however, been waiting for this for a long time, and now just as the inn-keeper was about to give a hearty tug, he cried: "Out of the sack, Cudgel!" Instantly the little cudgel came forth, and fell on the inn-keeper and gave him a sound thrashing.

The host cried for mercy; but the louder he cried, so much more heavily the cudgel beat the time on his back, until at length he fell to the ground exhausted. Then the turner said: "If thou dost not give back the table which covers itself, and the gold-ass, the dance shall begin afresh." — "Oh, no," cried the host, quite humbly, "I will gladly produce everything, only make the accursed kobold creep back into the sack." Then said the apprentice: "I will let mercy take the place of justice, but beware of getting into mischief again!" So he cried: "Into the sack, Cudgel!" and let him have rest.

Next morning the turner went home to his father with the wishing-table, and the gold-ass. The tailor rejoiced when he saw him once more, and asked him likewise what he had learned in foreign parts. "Dear father," said he, "I have become a turner." — "A skilled trade," said the father. "What hast thou brought back with thee from thy travels?"

"A precious thing, dear father," replied the son, "a cudgel in the sack." — "What!" cried the father, "a cudgel! That's worth thy trouble, indeed! From every tree thou can cut thyself one." — "But not one like this, dear father. If I say, 'Out of the sack, Cudgel!' the cudgel springs out and leads any one who means ill with me a weary dance, and never stops until he lies on the ground and prays for fair weather. Look you, with this cudgel have I got back the wishing-table and the gold-ass which the thievish inn-keeper took away from my brothers. Now let them both be sent for, and invite all our kinsmen. I will give them to eat and to drink, and will fill their pockets with gold into the bargain." The old tailor would not quite believe, but nevertheless got the relatives together. Then the turner spread a cloth in the room and led in the gold-ass, and said to his brother: "Now, dear brother, speak to him." The miller said: "Bricklebrit," and instantly the gold pieces fell down on the cloth like a thunder-shower, and the ass did not stop until every one of them had so much that he could carry no more. (I can see in thy face that thou also wouldst like to be there.)

106

Then the turner brought the little table, and said: "Now dear brother, speak to it." And scarcely had the carpenter said: "Table, cover thyself," than it was spread and amply covered with the most exquisite dishes. Then such a meal took place as the good tailor had never yet known in his house, and the whole party of kinsmen stayed together till far in the night, and were all merry and glad. The tailor locked away needle and thread, yard-measure and goose, in a press, and lived with his three sons in joy and splendour. (What, however, has become of the goat who was to blame for the tailor driving out his three sons? That I will tell thee. She was ashamed that she had a bald head, and ran to a fox's hole and crept into it. When the fox came home, he was met by two great eyes shining out of the darkness, and was terrified and ran away. A bear met him, and as the fox looked quite disturbed, he said: "What is the matter with thee, brother Fox, why dost thou look like that?" — "Ah," answered Redskin, "a fierce beast is in my cave and stared at me with its fiery eyes." — "We will soon drive him out," said the bear, and went with him to the cave and looked in, but when he saw the fiery eyes, fear seized on him likewise; he would have nothing to do with the furious beast, and took to his heels. The bee met him, and as she saw that he was ill at ease, she said: "Bear, thou art really pulling a very pitiful face; what has become of all thy gaiety?" — "It is all very well for thee to talk," replied the bear, "a furious beast with staring eyes is in Redskin's house, and we can't drive him out." The bee said: "Bear I pity thee, I am a poor weak creature whom thou wouldst not turn aside to look at, but still, I believe, I can help thee." She flew into the fox's cave, lighted on the goat's smoothly-shorn head, and stung her so violently, that she sprang up, crying "Meh, meh," and ran forth into the world as if mad, and to this hour no one knows where she has gone.)

Thumbling

Illustrated by Kyotarow Aoki

There was once a poor peasant who sat in the evening by the hearth and poked the fire, and his wife sat and span. Then said he: "How sad it is that we have no children! With us all is so quiet, and in other houses it is noisy and lively."

"Yes," replied the wife, and sighed, "even if we had only one, and it were quite small, and only as big as a thumb, I should be quite satisfied, and we would still love it with all our hearts." Now it so happened that the woman fell ill, and after seven months gave birth to a child, that was perfect in all its limbs, but no longer than a thumb. Then said they: "It is as we wished it to be, and it shall be our dear child;" and because of its size, they called it Thumbling. They did not let it want for food, but the child did not grow taller, but remained as it had been at the first, nevertheless it looked sensibly out of its eyes, and soon showed itself to be a wise and nimble creature, for everything it did turned out well.

One day the peasant was getting ready to go into the forest to cut wood, when he said as if to himself: "How I wish that there was any one who would bring the cart to me!" — "Oh father," cried Thumbling, "I will soon bring the cart, rely on that; it shall be in the forest at the appointed time." The man smiled and said: "How can that be done, thou art far too small to lead the horse by the reins?" "That's of no consequence, father, if my mother will only harness it, I shall sit in the horse's ear and call out to him how he is to go." — "Well," answered the man, "for once we will try it."

When the time came, the mother harnessed the horse, and placed Thumbling in its ear, and then the little creature cried: "Gee up, gee up!"

Then it went quite properly as if with its master, and the cart went the right way into the forest. It so happened that just as he was turning a corner, and the little one was crying: "Gee up," two strange men came towards him. "My word!" said one of them, "What is this? There is a cart coming, and a driver is calling to the horse and still he is not to be seen!" — "That can't be right," said the other, "we will follow the cart and see where it stops." The cart, however, drove right into the forest, and exactly to the place where the wood had been cut. When Thumbling saw his father, he cried to him: "Seest thou, father, here I am with the cart; now take me down." The father got hold of the horse with his left hand and with the right took his little son out of the ear. Thumbling sat down quite merrily on a straw, but when the two strange men saw him, they did not know what to say for astonishment. Then one of them took the other aside and said: "Hark, the little fellow would make our fortune if we exhibited him in a large town, for money. We will buy him." They went to the peasant and said: "Sell us the little man. He shall be well treated with us." — "No," replied the father, "he is the apple of my eye, and all the money in the world cannot buy him from me." Thumbling, however, when he heard of the bargain, had crept up the folds of his father's coat, placed himself on his shoulder, and whispered in his ear: "Father do give me away, I will soon come back again." Then the father parted with him to the two men for a handsome bit of money. "Where wilt thou sit?" they said to him. "Oh just set me on the rim of your hat, and then I can walk backwards and forwards and look at the country, and still not fall down." They did as he wished, and when Thumbling had taken leave of his father, they went away with him. They walked until it was dusk, and then the little fellow said: "Do take me down, I want to come down." The man took his hat off, and put the little fellow on the ground by the wayside, and he leapt and crept about a little between the sods, and then he suddenly slipped into a mouse-hole which he had sought out. "Good evening, gentlemen, just go home without me," he cried to them, and mocked them. They ran thither and stuck their sticks into the mouse-hole, but it was all lost labour. Thumbling crept still farther in, and as it soon became quite dark, they were forced to go home with their vexation and their empty purses.

When Thumbling saw that they were gone, he crept back out of the subterranean passage. "It is so dangerous to walk on the ground in the dark," said he; "how easily a neck or a leg is broken!" Fortunately he knocked against an empty snail-shell.

"Thank God!" said he. "In that I can pass the night in safety," and got into it. Not long afterwards, when he was just going to sleep, he heard two men go by, and one of them was saying: "How shall we contrive to get hold of the rich pastor's silver and gold?" — "I could tell thee that," cried Thumbling, interrupting them. "What was that?" said one of the thieves in fright, "I heard some one speaking." They stood still listening, and Thumbling spoke again, and said: "Take me with you, and I'll help you."

"But where art thou?" — "Just look on the ground, and observe from whence my voice comes," he replied. There the thieves at length found him, and lifted him up. "Thou little imp, how wilt thou help us?" they said. "A great deal," said he, "I will creep into the pastor's room through the iron bars, and will reach out to you whatever you want to have." — "Come then," they said, "and we will see what thou canst do." When they got to the pastor's house, Thumbling crept into the room, but instantly cried out with all his might: "Do you want to have everything that is here?" The thieves were alarmed, and said: "But do speak softly, so as not to waken any one!" Thumbling however, behaved as if he had not understood this, and cried again: "What do you want? Do you want to have everything that is here?" The cook, who slept in the next room, heard this and sat up in bed, and listened. The thieves, however, had in their fright run some distance away, but at last they took courage, and thought: "The little rascal wants to mock us." They came back and whispered to him: "Come, be serious, and reach something out to us." Then Thumbling again cried as loudly as he could: "I really will give you everything, just put your hands in." The maid who was listening, heard this quite distinctly, and jumped out of bed and rushed to the door. The thieves took flight, and ran as if the Wild Huntsman were behind them, but as the maid could not see anything, she went to strike a light. When she came to the place with it, Thumbling, unperceived, betook himself to the granary, and the maid, after she had examined every corner and found nothing, lay down in her bed again, and believed that, after all, she had only been dreaming with open eyes and ears.

Thumbling had climbed up among the hay and found a beautiful place to sleep in; there he intended to rest until day, and then go home again to his parents. But he had other things to go through. Truly, there is much affliction and misery in this world! When day dawned, the maid arose from her bed to feed the cows. Her first

113

walk was into the barn, where she laid hold of an armful of hay, and precisely that very one in which poor Thumbling was lying asleep. He, however, was sleeping so soundly that he was aware of nothing, and did not awake until he was in the mouth of the cow, who had picked him up with the hay. "Ah, heavens!" cried he, "how have I got into the fulling mill?" but he soon discovered where he was. Then it was necessary to be careful not to let himself go between the teeth and be dismembered, but he was nevertheless forced to slip down into the stomach with the hay. "In this little room the windows are forgotten," said he, "and no sun shines in, neither will a candle be brought." His quarters were especially unpleasing to him, and the worst was, more and more hay was always coming in by the door, and the space grew less and less. Then at length in his anguish, he cried as loud as he could: "Bring me no more fodder, bring me no more fodder." The maid was just milking the cow, and when she heard some one speaking, and saw no one, and perceived that it was the same voice that she had heard in the night, she was so terrified that she slipped off her stool, and spilt the milk. She ran in great haste to her master, and said: "Oh heavens, pastor, the cow has been speaking!" "Thou art mad," replied the pastor; but he went himself to the byre to see what was there. Hardly, however had he set his foot inside when Thumbling again cried: "Bring me no more fodder, bring me no more fodder." Then the pastor himself was alarmed, and thought that an evil spirit had gone into the cow, and ordered her to be killed. She was killed, but the stomach, in which Thumbling was, was thrown on the midden. Thumbling had great difficulty in working his way; however, he succeeded so far as to get some room, but just as he was going to thrust his head out, a new misfortune occurred. A hungry wolf ran thither, and swallowed the whole stomach at one gulp. Thumbling did not lose courage.

"Perhaps," thought he, "the wolf will listen to what I have got to say," and he called to him from out of his stomach, "Dear wolf, I know of a magnificent feast for you." — "Where is it to be had?" said the wolf. "In such and such a house; thou must creep into it through the kitchen-sink, and wilt find cakes, and bacon, and sausages, and as much of them as thou canst eat," and he described to him exactly his father's house. The wolf did not require to be told this twice, squeezed himself in at night through the sink, and ate to his heart's content in the larder. When he had eaten his fill, he wanted to go out again, but he had become so big that he could not go out by the same way. Thumbling had reckoned on this, and now began to make a violent noise in the wolf's body, and raged and screamed as loudly as he could. "Wilt thou be quiet," said the wolf, "thou wilt waken up the people!" — "Eh, what," replied the little fellow, "thou hast eaten thy fill, and I will make merry likewise," and began once more to scream with all his strength.

At last his father and mother were aroused by it, and ran to the room and looked in through the opening in the door. When they saw that a wolf was inside, they ran away, and the husband fetched his axe, and the wife the scythe. "Stay behind," said the man, when they entered the room. "When I have given him a blow, if he is not killed by it, thou must cut him down and hew his body to pieces." Then Thumbling heard his parents, voices and cried: "Dear father, I am here; I am in the wolf's body." Said the father, full of joy: "Thank God, our dear child has found us again," and bade the woman take away her scythe, that Thumbling might not be hurt with it. After that he raised his arm, and struck the wolf such a blow on his head that he fell down dead, and then they got knives and

scissors and cut his body open and drew the little fellow forth. "Ah," said the father, "what sorrow we have gone through for thy sake." — "Yes father, I have gone about the world a great deal. Thank heaven, I breathe fresh air again!" — "Where hast thou been, then?" — "Ah, father, I have been in a mouse's hole, in a cow's stomach, and then in a wolf's; now I will stay with you." — "And we will not sell thee again, no, not for all the riches in the world," said his parents, and they embraced and kissed their dear Thumbling. They gave him to eat and to drink, and had some new clothes made for him, for his own had been spoiled on his journey.

Jorinda & Joringel

Illustrated by Katrin Petursdottir

There was once an old castle in the midst of a large and thick forest, and in it an old woman who was a witch dwelt all alone. In the day-time she changed herself into a cat or a screech-owl, but in the evening she took her proper shape again as a human being. She could lure wild beasts and birds to her, and then she killed and boiled and roasted them. If any one came within one hundred paces of the castle he was obliged to stand still, and could not stir from the place until she bade him be free. But whenever an innocent maiden came within this circle, she changed her into a bird, and shut her up in a wicker-work cage, and carried the cage into a room in the castle. She had about seven thousand cages of rare birds in the castle.

Now, there was once a maiden who was called Jorinda, who was fairer than all other girls. She and a handsome youth named Joringel had promised to marry each other. They were still in the days of betrothal, and their greatest happiness was being together. One day in order that they might be able to talk together in quiet they went for a walk in the forest. "Take care," said Joringel, "that you do not go too near the castle."

It was a beautiful evening; the sun shone brightly between the trunks of the trees into the dark green of the forest, and the turtle-doves sang mournfully upon the young boughs of the birch-trees.

Jorinda wept now and then: she sat down in the sunshine and was sorrowful. Joringel was sorrowful too; they were as sad as if they were about to die. Then they looked around them, and were quite at a loss, for they did not know by which way they should go home. The sun was still half above the mountain and half set.

Joringel looked through the bushes, and saw the old walls of the castle close at hand. He was horror-stricken and filled with deadly fear. Jorinda was singing:

"My little bird, with the necklace red,
Sings sorrow, sorrow, sorrow,
He sings that the dove must soon be dead,
Sings sorrow, sor – jug, jug, jug."

Joringel looked for Jorinda. She was changed into a nightingale, and sang: "jug, jug, jug." A screech-owl with glowing eyes flew three times round about her, and three times cried: "To-whoo, to-whoo, to-whoo!" Joringel could not move: he stood there like a stone, and could neither weep nor speak, nor move hand or foot. The sun had now set. The owl flew into the thicket, and directly afterwards there came out of it a crooked old woman, yellow and lean, with large red eyes and a hooked nose, the point of which reached to her chin. She muttered to herself, caught the nightingale, and took it away in her hand.

120

Joringel could neither speak nor move from the spot; the nightingale was gone. At last the woman came back, and said in a hollow voice: "Greet thee, Zachiel. If the moon shines on the cage, Zachiel, let him loose at once." Then Joringel was freed. He fell on his knees before the woman and begged that she would give him back his Jorinda, but she said that he should never have her again, and went away. He called, he wept, he lamented, but all in vain: "Ah, what is to become of me?" Joringel went away, and at last came to a strange village; there he kept sheep for a long time. He often walked round and round the castle, but not too near to it. At last he dreamt one night that he found a blood-red flower, in the middle of which was a beautiful large pearl; that he picked the flower and went with it to the castle, and that everything he touched with the flower was freed from enchantment; he also dreamt that by means of it he recovered his Jorinda.

In the morning, when he awoke, he began to seek over hill and dale if he could find such a flower. He sought until the ninth day, and then, early in the morning, he found the blood-red flower. In the middle of it there was a large dew-drop, as big as the finest pearl.

Day and night he journeyed with this flower to the castle. When he was within a hundred paces of it he was not held fast, but walked on to the door. Joringel was full of joy; he touched the door with the flower, and it sprang open. He walked in through the courtyard, and listened for the sound of the birds. At last he heard it. He went on and found the room from whence it came, and there the witch was feeding the birds in the seven thousand cages.

When she saw Joringel she was angry, very angry, and scolded and spat poison and gall at him, but she could not come within two paces of him. He did not take any notice of her, but went and looked at the cages with the birds; but there were many hundred nightingales, how was he to find his Jorinda again?

Just then he saw the old woman quietly take away a cage with a bird in it, and go towards the door. Swiftly he sprang towards her, touched the cage with the flower, and also the old woman. She could now no longer bewitch any one; and Jorinda was standing there, clasping him round the neck, and she was as beautiful as ever. Then all the other birds were turned into maidens again, and he went home with his Jorinda, and they lived happily together for a long time.

Rapunzel

Illustrated by Pia Wall

There were once a man and a woman who had long in vain wished for a child. At length the woman hoped that God was about to grant her desire. These people had a little window at the back of their house from which a splendid garden could be seen, which was full of the most beautiful flowers and herbs. It was, however, surrounded by a high wall, and no one dared to go into it because it belonged to an enchantress, who had great power and was dreaded by all the world. One day the woman was standing by this window and looking down into the garden, when she saw a bed which was planted with the most beautiful rampion (rapunzel), and it looked so fresh and green that she longed for it, and had the greatest desire to eat some. This desire increased every day, and as she knew that she could not get any of it, she quite pined away, and looked pale and miserable. Then her husband was alarmed, and asked: "What aileth thee, dear wife?" — "Ah," she replied, "if I can't get some of the rampion, which is in the garden behind our house, to eat, I shall die."

The man, who loved her, thought: "Sooner than let thy wife die, bring her some of the rampion thyself, let it cost thee what it will." In the twilight of the evening, he clambered down over the wall into the garden of the enchantress, hastily clutched a handful of rampion, and took it to his wife. She at once made herself a salad of it, and ate it with much relish. She, however, liked it so much – so very much, that the next day she longed for it three times as much as before. If he was to have any rest, her husband must once more descend into the garden. In the gloom of evening, therefore, he let himself down again; but when he had clambered down the wall he was terribly afraid, for he saw the enchantress standing before him. "How canst thou dare," said she with angry look, "to descend into my garden and steal my rampion like a thief? Thou shalt suffer for it!" — "Ah," answered he, "let mercy take the place of justice, I only made up my mind to do it out of necessity. My wife saw your rampion from the window, and felt such a longing for it that she would have died if she had not got some to eat."

Then the enchantress allowed her anger to be softened, and said to him: "If the case be as thou sayest, I will allow thee to take away with thee as much rampion as thou wilt, only I make one condition, thou must give me the child which thy wife will bring into the world; it shall be well treated, and I will care for it like a mother." The man in his terror consented to everything, and when the woman was brought to bed, the enchantress appeared at once, gave the child the name of Rapunzel, and took it away with her.

Rapunzel grew into the most beautiful child beneath the sun. When she was twelve years old, the enchantress shut her into a tower, which lay in a forest, and had neither stairs nor door, but quite at the top was a little window. When the enchantress wanted to go in, she placed herself beneath it and cried:

"Rapunzel, Rapunzel, let down thy hair to me."

Rapunzel had magnificent long hair, fine as spun gold, and when she heard the voice of the enchantress she unfastened her braided tresses, wound them round one of the hooks of the window above, and then the hair fell twenty ells down, and the enchantress climbed up by it.

After a year or two, it came to pass that the King's son rode through the forest and went by the tower. Then he heard a song, which was so charming that he stood still and listened. This was Rapunzel, who in her solitude passed her time in letting her sweet voice resound. The King's son wanted to climb up to her, and looked for the door of the tower, but none was to be found. He rode home, but the singing had so deeply touched his heart, that every day he went out into the forest and listened to it. Once when he was thus standing behind a tree, he saw that an enchantress came there, and he heard how she cried:

"Rapunzel, Rapunzel, let down thy hair."

Then Rapunzel let down the braids of her hair, and the enchantress climbed up to her. "If that is the ladder by which one mounts, I will for once try my fortune," said he, and the next day when it began to grow dark, he went to the tower and cried:

"Rapunzel, Rapunzel, let down thy hair."

Immediately the hair fell down and the King's son climbed up. At first Rapunzel was terribly frightened when a man such as her eyes had never yet beheld, came to her; but the King's son began to talk to her quite like a friend, and told her that his heart had been so stirred that it had let him have no rest, and he had been forced to see her.

Then Rapunzel lost her fear, and when he asked her if she would take him for her husband, and she saw that he was young and handsome, she thought: "He will love me more than old Dame Gothel does;" and she said yes, and laid her hand in his. She said: "I will willingly go away with thee, but I do not know how to get down. Bring with thee a skein of silk every time that thou comest, and I will weave a ladder with it, and when that is ready I will descend, and thou wilt take me on thy horse."

They agreed that until that time he should come to her every evening, for the old woman came by day. The enchantress remarked nothing of this, until once Rapunzel said to her: "Tell me, Dame Gothel, how it happens that you are so much heavier for me to draw up than the young King's son – he is with me in a moment." — "Ah! thou wicked child," cried the enchantress "What do I hear thee say! I thought I had separated thee from all the world, and yet thou hast deceived me. In her anger she clutched Rapunzel's beautiful tresses, wrapped them twice round her left hand, seized a pair of scissors with the right, and snip, snap, they were cut off, and the lovely braids lay on the ground. And she was so pitiless that she took poor Rapunzel into a desert where she had to live in great grief and misery.

On the same day, however, that she cast out Rapunzel, the enchantress in the evening fastened the braids of hair which she had cut off, to the hook of the window, and when the King's son came and cried:

129

"Rapunzel, Rapunzel, let down thy hair,"

she let the hair down. The King's son ascended, but he did not find his dearest Rapunzel above, but the enchantress, who gazed at him with wicked and venomous looks. "Aha!" she cried mockingly, "Thou wouldst fetch thy dearest, but the beautiful bird sits no longer singing in the nest; the cat has got it, and will scratch out thy eyes as well. Rapunzel is lost to thee; thou wilt never see her more." The King's son was beside himself with pain, and in his despair he leapt down from the tower. He escaped with his life, but the thorns into which he fell, pierced his eyes. Then he wandered quite blind about the forest, ate nothing but roots and berries, and did nothing but lament and weep over the loss of his dearest wife. Thus he roamed about in misery for some years, and at length came to the desert where Rapunzel, with the twins to which she had given birth, a boy and a girl, lived in wretchedness. He heard a voice, and it seemed so familiar to him that he went towards it, and when he approached, Rapunzel knew him and fell on his neck and wept. Two of her tears wetted his eyes and they grew clear again, and he could see with them as before. He led her to his kingdom where he was joyfully received, and they lived for a long time afterwards, happy and contented.

Briar-Rose

Illustrated by Erotic Dragon

A long time ago there were a King and Queen who said every day: "Ah, if only we had a child!" but they never had one. But it happened that once when the Queen was bathing, a frog crept out of the water on to the land, and said to her: "Your wish shall be fulfilled; before a year has gone by, you shall have a daughter."

What the frog had said came true, and the Queen had a little girl who was so pretty that the King could not contain himself for joy, and ordered a great feast. He invited not only his kindred, friends and acquaintance, but also the Wise Women, in order that they might be kind and well-disposed towards the child. There were thirteen of them in his kingdom, but, as he had only twelve golden plates for them to eat out of, one of them had to be left at home.

The feast was held with all manner of splendour and when it came to an end the Wise Women bestowed their magic gifts upon the baby: one gave virtue, another beauty, a third riches, and so on with everything in the world that one can wish for.

When eleven of them had made their promises, suddenly the thirteenth came in. She wished to avenge herself for not having been invited, and without greeting, or even looking at any one, she cried with a loud voice: "The King's daughter shall in her fifteenth year prick herself with a spindle, and fall down dead." And, without saying a word more, she turned round and left the room.

They were all shocked; but the twelfth, whose good wish still remained unspoken, came forward, and as she could not undo the evil sentence, but only soften it, she said: "It shall not be death, but a deep sleep of a hundred years, into which the princess shall fall."

The King, who would fain keep his dear child from the misfortune, gave orders that every spindle in the whole kingdom should be burnt. Meanwhile the gifts of the Wise Women were plenteously fulfilled on the young girl, for she was so beautiful, modest, good-natured, and wise, that everyone who saw her was bound to love her. It happened that on the very day when she was fifteen years old, the King and Queen were not at home, and the maiden was left in the palace quite alone. So she went round into all sorts of places, looked into rooms and bed-chambers just as she liked, and at last came to an old tower. She climbed up the narrow winding-staircase, and reached a little door. A rusty key was in the lock, and when she turned it the door sprang open, and there in a little room sat an old woman with a spindle, busily spinning her flax.

"Good day, old dame," said the King's daughter; "what are you doing there?" — "I am spinning," said the old woman, and nodded her head. "What sort of thing is that, that rattles round so merrily?" said the girl, and she took the spindle and wanted to spin too. But scarcely had she touched the spindle when the magic decree was fulfilled, and she pricked her finger with it.

134

And, in the very moment when she felt the prick, she fell down upon the bed that stood there, and lay in a deep sleep. And this sleep extended over the whole palace; the King and Queen who had just come home, and had entered the great hall, began to go to sleep, and the whole of the court with them. The horses, too, went to sleep in the stable, the dogs in the yard, the pigeons upon the roof, the flies on the wall; even the fire that was flaming on the hearth became quiet and slept, the roast meat left off frizzling, and the cook, who was just going to pull the hair of the scullery boy, because he had forgotten something, let him go, and went to sleep. And the wind fell, and on the trees before the castle not a leaf moved again.

But round about the castle there began to grow a hedge of thorns, which every year became higher, and at last grew close up round the castle and all over it, so that there was nothing of it to be seen, not even the flag upon the roof. But the story of the beautiful sleeping "Briar-rose," for so the princess was named, went about the country, so that from time to time kings' sons came and tried to get through the thorny hedge into the castle.

But they found it impossible, for the thorns held fast together, as if they had hands, and the youths were caught in them, could not get loose again, and died a miserable death.

After long, long years a King's son came again to that country, and heard an old man talking about the thorn-hedge, and that a castle was said to stand behind it in which a wonderfully beautiful princess, named Briar-rose, had been asleep for a hundred years; and that the King and Queen and the whole court were asleep likewise. He had heard, too, from his grandfather, that many kings' sons had already come, and had tried to get through the thorny hedge, but they had remained sticking fast in it, and had died a pitiful death. Then the youth said: "I am not afraid, I will go and see the beautiful Briar-rose." The good old man might dissuade him as he would, he did not listen to his words.

But by this time the hundred years had just passed, and the day had come when Briar-rose was to awake again. When the King's son came near to the thorn-hedge, it was nothing but large and beautiful flowers, which parted from each other of their own accord, and let him pass unhurt, then they closed again behind him like a hedge. In the castle-yard he saw the horses and the spotted hounds lying asleep; on the roof sat the pigeons with their heads under their wings. And when he entered the house, the flies were asleep upon the wall, the cook in the kitchen was still holding out his hand to seize the boy, and the maid was sitting by the black hen which she was going to pluck.

He went on farther, and in the great hall he saw the whole of the court lying asleep, and up by the throne lay the King and Queen.

Then he went on still farther, and all was so quiet that a breath could be heard, and at last he came to the tower, and opened the door into the little room where Briar-rose was sleeping. There she lay, so beautiful that he could not turn his eyes away; and he stooped down and gave her a kiss. But as soon as he kissed her, Briar-rose opened her eyes and awoke, and looked at him quite sweetly.

Then they went down together, and the King awoke, and the Queen, and the whole court, and looked at each other in great astonishment. And the horses in the court-yard stood up and shook themselves; the hounds jumped up and wagged their tails; the pigeons upon the roof pulled out their heads from under their

wings, looked round, and flew into the open country; the flies on the wall crept again; the fire in the kitchen burned up and flickered and cooked the meat; the joint began to turn and frizzle again, and the cook gave the boy such a box on the ear that he screamed, and the maid plucked the fowl ready for the spit.

And then the marriage of the King's son with Briar-rose was celebrated with all splendour, and they lived contented to the end of their days.

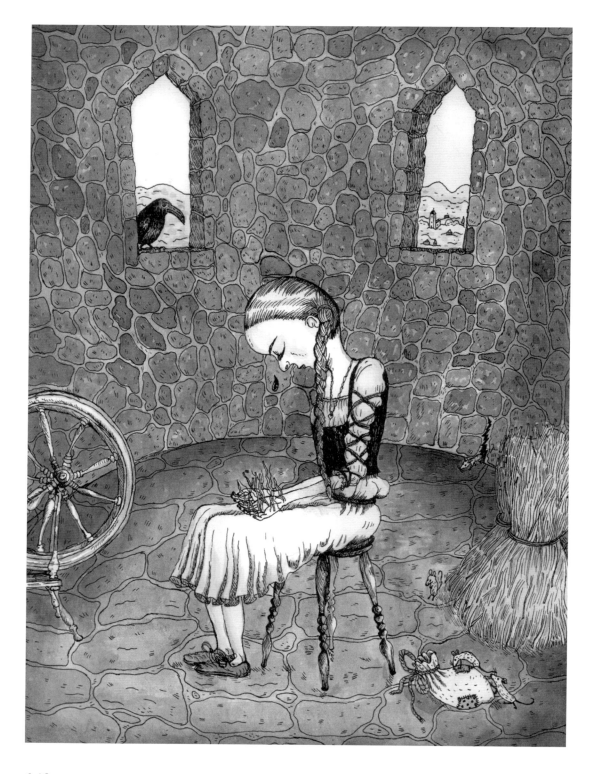

140

Rumpelstiltskin

Illustrated by Emma Åkerman

Once there was a miller who was poor, but who had a beautiful daughter. Now it happened that he had to go and speak to the King, and in order to make himself appear important he said to him: "I have a daughter who can spin straw into gold." The King said to the miller: "That is an art which pleases me well; if your daughter is as clever as you say, bring her to-morrow to my palace, and I will try what she can do."

And when the girl was brought to him he took her into a room which was quite full of straw, gave her a spinning-wheel and a reel, and said, "Now set to work, and if by to-morrow morning early you have not spun this straw into gold during the night, you must die." Thereupon he himself locked up the room, and left her in it alone. So there sat the poor miller's daughter, and for the life of her could not tell what to do; she had no idea how straw could be spun into gold, and she grew more and more miserable, until at last she began to weep.

But all at once the door opened, and in came a little man, and said: "Good evening, Mistress Miller; why are you crying so?" — "Alas!" answered the girl, "I have to spin straw into gold, and I do not know how to do it." — "What will you give me," said the manikin, "if I do it for you?" — "My necklace," said the girl. The little man took the necklace, seated himself in front of the wheel, and "whirr, whirr, whirr," three turns, and the reel was full; then he put another on, and whirr, whirr, whirr, three times round, and the second was full too. And so it went on until the morning, when all the straw was spun, and all the reels were full of gold. By daybreak the King was already there, and when he saw the gold he was astonished and delighted, but his heart became only more greedy. He had the miller's daughter taken into another room full of straw, which was much larger, and commanded her to spin that also in one night if she valued her life.

The girl knew not how to help herself, and was crying, when the door again opened, and the little man appeared, and said: "What will you give me if I spin that straw into gold for you?" — "The ring on my finger," answered the girl. The little man took the ring, again began to turn the wheel, and by morning had spun all the straw into glittering gold.

The King rejoiced beyond measure at the sight, but still he had not gold enough; and he had the miller's daughter taken into a still larger room full of straw, and said: "You must spin this, too, in the course of this night; but if you succeed, you shall be my wife." — "Even if she be a miller's daughter," thought he, "I could not find a richer wife in the whole world."

When the girl was alone the manikin came again for the third time, and said: "What will you give me if I spin the straw for you this time also?" — "I have nothing left that I could give," answered the girl. "Then promise me, if you should become Queen, your first child." — "Who knows whether that will ever happen?" thought the miller's daughter; and, not knowing how else to help herself in this strait, she promised the manikin what he wanted, and for that he once more span the straw into gold.

142

And when the King came in the morning, and found all as he had wished, he took her in marriage, and the pretty miller's daughter became a Queen.

A year after, she had a beautiful child, and she never gave a thought to the manikin. But suddenly he came into her room, and said: "Now give me what you promised." The Queen was horror-struck, and offered the manikin all the riches of the kingdom if he would leave her the child. But the manikin said: "No, something that is living is dearer to me than all the treasures in the world." Then the Queen began to weep and cry, so that the manikin pitied her. "I will give you three days' time," said he, "if by that time you find out my name, then shall you keep your child."

So the Queen thought the whole night of all the names that she had ever heard, and she sent a messenger over the country to inquire, far and wide, for any other names that there might be. When the manikin came the next day, she began with Caspar, Melchior, Balthazar, and said all the names she knew, one after another; but to every one the little man said: "That is not my name." On the second day she had inquiries made in the neighborhood as to the names of the people

there, and she repeated to the manikin the most uncommon and curious. "Perhaps your name is Shortribs, or Sheepshanks, or Laceleg?" but he always answered, "That is not my name."

On the third day the messenger came back again, and said: "I have not been able to find a single new name, but as I came to a high mountain at the end of the forest, where the fox and the hare bid each other good night, there I saw a little house, and before the house a fire was burning, and round about the fire quite a ridiculous little man was jumping: he hopped upon one leg, and shouted:

"Today I bake, tomorrow brew,
The next I'll have the young Queen's child.
Ha! glad am I that no one knew
That Rumpelstiltskin I am styled."

You may think how glad the Queen was when she heard the name! And when soon afterwards the little man came in, and asked: "Now, Mistress Queen, what is my name?" at first she said, "Is your name Conrad?" — "No." — "Is your name Harry?" — "No." — "Perhaps your name is Rumpelstiltskin?"

"The devil has told you that! the devil has told you that!" cried the little man, and in his anger he plunged his right foot so deep into the earth that his whole leg went in; and then in rage he pulled at his left leg so hard with both hands that he tore himself in two.

Story of the Youth Who Went Forth to Learn What Fear Was

Illustrated by Hendrik Hellige

A certain father had two sons, the elder of whom was smart and sensible, and could do everything, but the younger was stupid and could neither learn nor understand anything, and when people saw him they said: "There's a fellow who will give his father some trouble!" When anything had to be done, it was always the elder who was forced to do it; but if his father bade him fetch anything when it was late, or in the night-time, and the way led through the churchyard, or any other dismal place, he answered "Oh, no, father, I'll not go there, it makes me shudder!" for he was afraid. Or when stories were told by the fire at night which made the flesh creep, the listeners sometimes said "Oh, it makes us shudder!" The younger sat in a corner and listened with the rest of them, and could not imagine what they could mean. "They are always saying 'it makes me shudder, it makes me shudder!' It does not make me shudder," thought he. "That, too, must be an art of which I understand nothing."

Now it came to pass that his father said to him one day "Hearken to me, thou fellow in the corner there, thou art growing tall and strong, and thou too must learn something by which thou canst earn thy living. Look how thy brother works, but thou dost not even earn thy salt." — "Well, father," he replied, "I am quite willing to learn something – indeed, if it could but be managed, I should like to learn how to shudder. I don't understand that at all yet." The elder brother smiled when he heard that, and thought to himself: "Good God, what a blockhead that brother of mine is! He will never be good for anything as long as he lives. He who wants to be a sickle must bend himself betimes."

The father sighed, and answered him "thou shalt soon learn what it is to shudder, but thou wilt not earn thy bread by that."

Soon after this the sexton came to the house on a visit, and the father bewailed his trouble, and told him how his younger son was so backward in every respect that he knew nothing and learnt nothing. "Just think," said he, "when I asked him how he was going to earn his bread, he actually wanted to learn to shudder." — "If that be all," replied the sexton, "he can learn that with me. Send him to me, and I will soon polish him." The father was glad to do it, for he thought: "It will train the boy a little." The sexton therefore took him into his house, and he had to ring the bell. After a day or two, the sexton awoke him at midnight, and bade him arise and go up into the church tower and ring the bell. "Thou shalt soon learn what shuddering is," thought he, and secretly went there before him; and when the boy was at the top of the tower and turned round, and was just going to take hold of the bell rope, he saw a white figure standing on the stairs opposite the sounding hole. "Who is there?" cried he, but the figure made no reply, and did not move or stir. "Give an answer," cried the boy, "or take thy self off, thou hast no business here at night."

The sexton, however, remained standing motionless that the boy might think he was a ghost. The boy cried a second time: "What do you want here? – speak if thou art an honest fellow, or I will throw thee down the steps!" The sexton thought: "he can't intend to be as bad as his words," uttered no sound and stood as if he were made of stone. Then the boy called to him for the third time, and as that was also to no purpose, he ran against him and pushed the ghost down the stairs, so that it fell down ten steps and remained lying there in a corner. Thereupon he rang the bell, went home, and without saying a word went to bed, and fell asleep. The sexton's wife waited a long time for her husband, but he did not come back. At length she became uneasy, and wakened the boy, and asked: "Dost thou not know where my husband is? He climbed up the tower before thou didst." — "No, I don't know," replied the boy, "but some one was standing by the sounding hole on the other side of the steps, and as he would neither give an answer nor go away, I took him for a scoundrel, and threw him downstairs, just go there and you will see if it was he. I should be sorry if it were." The woman ran away and found her husband, who was lying moaning in the corner, and had broken his leg.

She carried him down, and then with loud screams she hastened to the boy's father. "Your boy," cried she, "has been the cause of a great misfortune! He has thrown my husband down the steps and made him break his leg. Take the good-for-nothing fellow away from our house." The father was terrified, and ran thither and scolded the boy. "What wicked tricks are these?" said he, "the devil must have put this into thy head." — "Father," he replied, "do listen to me. I am quite innocent. He was standing there by night like one who is intending to do some evil. I did not know who it was, and I entreated him three times either to speak or to go away." — "Ah," said the father, "I have nothing but unhappiness with you. Go out of my sight. I will see thee no more." — "Yes, father, right willingly, wait only until it is day. Then will I go forth and learn how to shudder, and then I shall, at any rate, understand one art which will support me." — "Learn what thou wilt," spake the father, "it is all the same to me. Here are fifty thalers for thee. Take these and go into the wide world, and tell no one from whence thou comest, and who is thy father, for I have reason to be ashamed of thee." — "Yes, father, it shall be as you will. If you desire nothing more than that, I can easily keep it in mind."

When day dawned, therefore, the boy put his fifty thalers into his pocket, and went forth on the great highway, and continually said to himself: "If I could but shudder! If I could but shudder!" Then a man approached who heard this conversation which the youth was holding with himself, and when they had walked a little farther to where they could see the gallows, the man said to him: "Look, there is the tree where seven men have married the ropemaker's daughter, and are now learning how to fly. Sit down below it, and wait till night comes, and you will soon learn how to shudder." — "If that is all that is wanted," answered the youth, "it is easily done; but if I learn how to shudder as fast as that, thou shalt have my fifty thalers. Just come back to me early in the morning." Then the youth went to the gallows, sat down below it, and waited till evening came. And as he was cold, he lighted himself a fire, but at midnight the wind blew so sharply that in spite of his fire, he could not get warm. And as the wind knocked the hanged men against each other, and they moved backwards and forwards, he thought to himself "Thou shiverest below by the fire, but how those up above must freeze and suffer!" And as he felt pity for them, he raised the ladder, and climbed up, unbound one of them after the other, and brought down all seven. Then he stirred the fire, blew it, and set them all round it to warm themselves. But they sat there and did not stir, and the fire caught their clothes. So he said: "Take care, or I will hang you up again." The dead men, however, did not hear, but were quite silent, and let their rags go on burning. On this he grew angry, and said: "If you will not take care, I cannot help you, I will not be burnt with you," and he hung them up again each in his turn. Then he sat down by his fire and fell asleep, and the next morning the man came to him and wanted to have the fifty thalers, and said: "Well, dost thou know how to shudder?" — "No," answered he, "how was I to get to know? Those fellows up there did not open their mouths, and were so stupid that they let the few old rags which they had on their bodies get burnt." Then the man saw that he would not get the fifty thalers that day, and went away saying: "One of this kind has never come my way before."

The youth likewise went his way, and once more began to mutter to himself: "Ah, if I could but shudder! Ah, if I could but shudder!" A waggoner who was striding behind him heard that and asked: "Who are you?" — "I don't know," answered the youth. Then the waggoner asked: "From whence comest thou?" — "I know not." "Who is thy father?" — "That I may not tell thee." — "What is it that thou art al-

152

ways muttering between thy teeth." — "Ah," replied the youth, "I do so wish I could shudder, but no one can teach me how to do it." — "Give up thy foolish chatter," said the waggoner. "Come, go with me, I will see about a place for thee." The youth went with the waggoner, and in the evening they arrived at an inn where they wished to pass the night. Then at the entrance of the room the youth again said quite loudly: "If I could but shudder! If I could but shudder!" The host who heard this, laughed and said: "If that is your desire, there ought to be a good opportunity for you here." — "Ah, be silent," said the hostess, "so many inquisitive persons have already lost their lives, it would be a pity and a shame if such beautiful eyes as these should never see the daylight again."

But the youth said: "However difficult it may be, I will learn it and for this purpose indeed have I journeyed forth." He let the host have no rest, until the latter told him, that not far from thence stood a haunted castle where any one could very easily learn what shuddering was, if he would but watch in it for three nights. The King had promised that he who would venture should have his daughter to wife, and she was the most beautiful maiden the sun shone on. Great treasures likewise lay in the castle, which were guarded by evil spirits, and these treasures would then be freed, and would make a poor man rich enough. Already many men had gone into the castle, but as yet none had come out again. Then the youth went next morning to the King and said if he were allowed he would watch three nights in the haunted castle. The King looked at him, and as the youth pleased him, he said: "Thou mayest ask for three things to take into the castle with thee, but they must be things without life." Then he answered: "Then I ask for a fire, a turning lathe, and a cutting-board with the knife." The King had these things carried into the castle for him during the day. When night was drawing near, the youth went up and made himself a bright fire in one of the rooms, placed the cutting-board and knife beside it, and seated himself by the turning-lathe. "Ah, if I could but shudder!" said he, "but I shall not learn it here either." Towards midnight he was about to poke his fire, and as he was blowing it, something cried suddenly from one corner: "Au, miau! How cold we are!" — "You simpletons!" cried he, "what are you crying about? If you are cold, come and take a seat by the fire and warm yourselves." And when he had said that, two great black cats came with one tremendous leap and sat down on each side of him, and looked savagely at him with their fiery eyes. After a short time, when they had warmed themselves, they said: "Comrade, shall we have a game at cards?" — "Why not?" he replied, "but just show me your paws." Then they stretched out their claws. "Oh," said he, "what long nails you have! Wait, I must first cut them for you." Thereupon he seized them by the throats, put them on the cutting-board and screwed their feet fast. "I have looked at your fingers," said he, "and my fancy for card-playing has gone," and he struck them dead and threw them out into the water. But when he had made away with these two, and was about to sit down again by his fire, out from every hole and corner came black cats and black dogs with red-hot chains, and more and more of them came until he could no longer stir, and they yelled horribly, and got on his fire, pulled it to pieces, and tried to put it out. He watched them for a while quietly, but at last when they were going too far, he seized his cutting-knife, and cried: "Away with ye, vermin," and began to cut them down. Part of them ran away, the others he killed, and threw out into the fish-pond. When he came back he fanned the embers of his fire again and warmed himself. And as he thus sat, his eyes would keep open no longer, and he

154

felt a desire to sleep. Then he looked round and saw a great bed in the corner. "That is the very thing for me," said he, and got into it. When he was just going to shut his eyes, however, the bed began to move of its own accord, and went over the whole of the castle. "That's right," said he, "but go faster." Then the bed rolled on as if six horses were harnessed to it, up and down, over thresholds and steps, but suddenly hop, hop, it turned over upside down, and lay on him like a mountain. But he threw quilts and pillows up in the air, got out and said: "Now any one who likes, may drive," and lay down by his fire, and slept till it was day. In the morning the King came, and when he saw him lying there on the ground, he thought the evil spirits had killed him and he was dead. Then said he: "After all it is a pity, he is a handsome man." The youth heard it, got up, and said: "It has not come to that yet." Then the King was astonished, but very glad, and asked how he had fared. "Very well indeed," answered he; "one night is past, the two others will get over likewise." Then he went to the innkeeper, who opened his eyes very wide, and said: "I never expected to see thee alive again! Hast thou learnt how to shudder yet?" — "No," said he, "it is all in vain. If some one would but tell me."

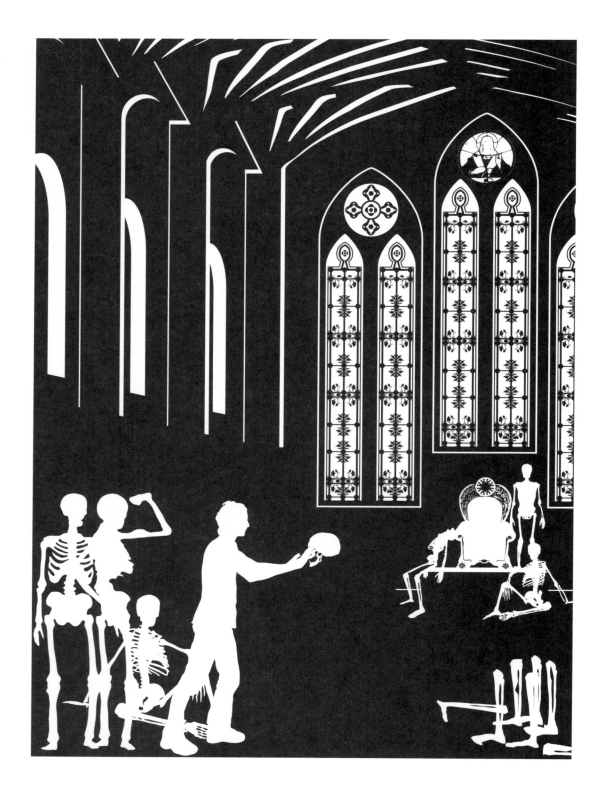

156

The second night he again went up into the old castle, sat down by the fire, and once more began his old song: "If I could but shudder." When midnight came, an uproar and noise of tumbling about was heard; at first it was low, but it grew louder and louder. Then it was quiet for awhile, and at length with a loud scream, half a man came down the chimney and fell before him. "Hollo!" cried he, "another half belongs to this. This is too little!" Then the uproar began again, there was a roaring and howling, and the other half fell down likewise. "Wait," said he, "I will just blow up the fire a little for thee." When he had done that and looked round again, the two pieces were joined together, and a frightful man was sitting in his place. "That is no part of our bargain," said the youth, "the bench is mine." The man wanted to push him away; the youth, however, would not allow that, but thrust him off with all his strength, and seated himself again in his own place. Then still more men fell down, one after the other; they brought nine dead men's legs and two skulls, and set them up and played at nine-pins with them. The youth also wanted to play and said "Hark you, can I join you?" — "Yes, if thou hast any money." — "Money enough," replied he, "but your balls are not quite round." Then he took the skulls and put them in the lathe and turned them till they were round. "There, now, they will roll better!" said he. "Hurrah! Now it goes merrily!" He played with them and lost some of his money, but when it struck twelve, everything vanished from his sight. He lay down and quietly fell asleep. Next morning the King came to inquire after him. "How has it fared with you this time?" asked he. "I have been playing at nine-pins," he answered, "and have lost a couple of farthings." — "Hast thou not shuddered then?" — "Eh, what?" said he, "I have made merry. If I did but know what it was to shudder!"

The third night he sat down again on his bench and said quite sadly: "If I could but shudder." When it grew late, six tall men came in and brought a coffin. Then said he: "Ha, ha, that is certainly my little cousin, who died only a few days ago," and he beckoned with his finger, and cried "Come, little cousin, come." They placed the coffin on the ground, but he went to it and took the lid off, and a dead man lay therein. He felt his face, but it was cold as ice. "Stop," said he, "I will warm thee a little," and went to the fire and warmed his hand and laid it on the dead man's face, but he remained cold. Then he took him out, and sat down by the fire and laid him on his breast and rubbed his arms that the blood might circulate again. As this also did no good, he thought to himself "When two people lie in bed together, they warm each other," and carried him to the bed, covered him over and lay down by him. After a short time the dead man became warm too, and began to move. Then said the youth: "See, little cousin, have I not warmed thee?" The dead man, however, got up and cried: "Now will I strangle thee."

"What!" said he, "is that the way thou thankest me? Thou shalt at once go into thy coffin again," and he took him up, threw him into it, and shut the lid. Then came the six men and carried him away again. "I cannot manage to shudder," said he. "I shall never learn it here as long as I live."

Then a man entered who was taller than all others, and looked terrible. He was old, however, and had a long white beard. "Thou wretch," cried he, "thou shalt soon learn what it is to shudder, for thou shalt die." — "Not so fast," replied the youth. "If I am to die, I shall have to have a say in it." — "I will soon seize thee," said the fiend. "Softly, softly, do not talk so big. I am as strong as thou art, and perhaps even stronger." — "We shall see," said the old man. "If thou art stronger, I will let thee go – come, we will try." Then he led him by dark passages to a smith's forge, took an axe, and with one blow struck an anvil into the ground. "I can do better than that," said the youth, and went to the other anvil. The old man placed himself near and wanted to look on, and his white beard hung down. Then the youth seized the axe, split the anvil with one blow, and struck the old man's beard in with it. "Now I have thee," said the youth. "Now it is thou who will have to die." Then he seized an iron bar and beat the old man till he moaned and entreated him to stop, and he would give him great riches. The youth drew out the axe and let him go. The old man led him back into the castle, and in a cellar showed him three chests full of gold. "Of these," said he, "one part is for the poor, the other for the king, the third is thine." In the meantime it struck twelve, and the spirit disappeared; the youth, therefore, was left in darkness. "I shall still be able to find my way out," said he, and felt about, found the way into the room, and slept there by his fire. Next morning the King came and said "Now thou must have learnt what shuddering is?" — "No," he answered; "what can it be? My dead cousin was here, and a bearded man came and showed me a great deal of money down below, but no one told me what it was to shudder." — "Then," said the King, "thou hast de-

160

livered the castle, and shalt marry my daughter." — "That is all very well," said he, "but still I do not know what it is to shudder."

Then the gold was brought up and the wedding celebrated; but howsoever much the young king loved his wife, and however happy he was, he still said always "If I could but shudder – if I could but shudder." And at last she was angry at this. Her waiting-maid said: "I will find a cure for him; he shall soon learn what it is to shudder." She went out to the stream which flowed through the garden, and had a whole bucketful of gudgeons brought to her. At night when the young king was sleeping, his wife was to draw the clothes off him and empty the bucketful of cold water with the gudgeons in it over him, so that the little fishes would sprawl about him. When this was done, he woke up and cried "Oh, what makes me shudder so? – what makes me shudder so, dear wife? Ah! now I know what it is to shudder!"

162

Little Snow-White

Illustrated by Kinpro

Once upon a time in the middle of winter, when the flakes of snow were falling like feathers from the sky, a queen sat at a window sewing, and the frame of the window was made of black ebony. And whilst she was sewing and looking out of the window at the snow, she pricked her finger with the needle, and three drops of blood fell upon the snow.

And the red looked pretty upon the white snow, and she thought to herself: "Would that I had a child as white as snow, as red as blood, and as black as the wood of the window-frame."

Soon after that she had a little daughter, who was as white as snow, and as red as blood, and her hair was as black as ebony; and she was therefore called Little Snow-White. And when the child was born, the Queen died.

After a year had passed the King took to himself another wife. She was a beautiful woman, but proud and haughty, and she could not bear that anyone else should surpass her in beauty. She had a wonderful looking-glass, and when she stood in front of it and looked at herself in it, and said:

"Looking-glass, looking-glass, on the wall, who in this land is the fairest of all?"

the looking-glass answered: "Thou, O Queen, art the fairest of all!"

Then she was satisfied, for she knew that the looking-glass spoke the truth. But Snow-White was growing up, and grew more and more beautiful; and when she was seven years old she was as beautiful as the day, and more beautiful than the Queen herself. And once when the Queen asked her looking-glass:

"Looking-glass, looking-glass, on the wall, who in this land is the fairest of all?"

it answered: "Thou art fairer than all who are here, Lady Queen."
But more beautiful still is Snow-White, as I ween."

Then the Queen was shocked, and turned yellow and green with envy. From that hour, whenever she looked at Snow-White, her heart heaved in her breast, she hated the girl so much.

And envy and pride grew higher and higher in her heart like a weed, so that she had no peace day or night. She called a huntsman, and said: "Take the child away into the forest; I will no longer have her in my sight. Kill her, and bring me back her heart as a token." The huntsman obeyed, and took her away; but when he had drawn his knife, and was about to pierce Snow-White's innocent heart, she began to weep, and said: "Ah dear huntsman, leave me my life! I will run away into the wild forest, and never come home again."

And as she was so beautiful the huntsman had pity on her and said: "Run away, then, you poor child." — "The wild beasts will soon have devoured you," thought he, and yet it seemed as if a stone had been rolled from his heart since it was no longer needful for him to kill her. And as a young boar just then came running by he stabbed it, and cut out its heart and took it to the Queen as proof that the child was dead. The cook had to salt this, and the wicked Queen ate it, and thought she had eaten the heart of Snow-White.

But now the poor child was all alone in the great forest, and so terrified that she looked at every leaf of every tree, and did not know what to do. Then she began to run, and ran over sharp stones and through thorns, and the wild beasts ran past her, but did her no harm.

She ran as long as her feet would go until it was almost evening; then she saw a little cottage and went into it to rest herself. Everything in the cottage was small, but neater and cleaner than can be told. There was a table on which was a white cover, and seven little plates, and on each plate a little spoon; more-over, there were seven little knives and forks, and seven little mugs. Against the wall stood seven little beds side by side, and covered with snow-white coun-terpanes.

164

Little Snow-White was so hungry and thirsty that she ate some vegetables and bread from each plate and drank a drop of wine out of each mug, for she did not wish to take all from one only. Then, as she was so tired, she laid herself down on one of the little beds, but none of them suited her; one was too long, another too short, but at last she found that the seventh one was right, and so she remained in it, said a prayer and went to sleep.

When it was quite dark the owners of the cottage came back; they were seven dwarfs who dug and delved in the mountains for ore. They lit their seven candles, and as it was now light within the cottage they saw that someone had been there, for everything was not in the same order in which they had left it.

The first said: "Who has been sitting on my chair?" — The second: "Who has been eating off my plate?" — The third: "Who has been taking some of my bread?" The fourth: "Who has been eating my vegetables?" — The fifth: "Who has been using my fork?" — The sixth: "Who has been cutting with my knife?" — The seventh: "Who has been drinking out of my mug?"

Then the first looked round and saw that there was a little hole on his bed, and he said: "Who has been getting into my bed?" The others came up and each called out: "Somebody has been lying in my bed too." But the seventh when he looked at his bed saw little Snow-White, who was lying asleep therein. And he called the others, who came running up, and they cried out with astonishment, and brought their seven little candles and let the light fall on little Snow-White. "Oh, heavens! oh, heavens!" cried they, "what a lovely child!" and they were so glad that they did not wake her up, but let her sleep on in the bed. And the seventh dwarf slept with his companions, one hour with each, and so got through the night.

When it was morning little Snow-White awoke, and was frightened when she saw the seven dwarfs. But they were friendly and asked her what her name was. "My name is Snow-White," she answered. "How have you come to our house?" said the dwarfs. Then she told them that her step-mother had wished to have her killed, but that the huntsman had spared her life, and that she had run for the whole day, until at last she had found their dwelling. The dwarfs said: "If you will take care of our house, cook, make the beds, wash, sew, and knit, and if you will keep everything neat and clean, you can stay with us and you shall want for nothing." — "Yes," said Snow-White, "with all my heart," and she stayed with them. She kept the house in order for them; in the mornings they went to the mountains and looked for copper and gold, in the evenings they came back, and then their supper had to be ready. The girl was alone the whole day, so the good dwarfs warned her and said: "Beware of your step-mother, she will soon know that you are here; be sure to let no one come in." But the Queen, believing that she had eaten Snow-White's heart, could not but think that she was again the first and most beautiful of all; and she went to her looking-glass and said:

"Looking-glass, looking-glass, on the wall, who in this land is the fairest of all?"

and the glass answered: "Oh, Queen, thou art fairest of all I see,
But over the hills, where the seven dwarfs dwell,
Snow-White is still alive and well,
And none is so fair as she."

Then she was astounded, for she knew that the looking-glass never spoke falsely, and she knew that the huntsman had betrayed her, and that little Snow-White was still alive. And so she thought and thought again how she might kill her, for so long as she was not the fairest in the whole land, envy let her have no rest.

And when she had at last thought of something to do, she painted her face, and dressed herself like an old pedler-woman, and no one could have known her. In this disguise she went over the seven mountains to the seven dwarfs, and knocked at the door and cried: "Pretty things to sell, very cheap, very cheap." Little Snow-White looked out of the window and called out: "Good-day my good woman, what have you to sell?" — "Good things, pretty things," she answered, "stay-laces of all colours," and she pulled out one which was woven of bright-coloured silk. "I may let the worthy old woman in," thought Snow-White, and she unbolted the door and bought the pretty laces. "Child," said the old woman, "what a fright you look; come, I will lace you properly for once."

Snow-White had no suspicion, but stood before her, and let herself be laced with the new laces. But the old woman laced so quickly and so tightly that Snow-White lost her breath and fell down as if dead. "Now I am the most beautiful," said the Queen to herself, and ran away.

Not long afterwards, in the evening, the seven dwarfs came home, but how shocked they were when they saw their dear little Snow-White lying on the ground, and that she neither stirred nor moved, and seemed to be dead. They lifted her up, and, as they saw that she was laced too tightly, they cut the laces; then she began to breathe a little, and after a while came to life again.

When the dwarfs heard what had happened they said: "The old pedler-woman was no one else than the wicked Queen; take care and let no one come in when we are not with you." But the wicked woman when she had reached home went in front of the glass and asked:

"Looking-glass, looking-glass, on the wall, who in this land is the fairest of all?"

and it answered as before: "Oh, Queen, thou art fairest of all I see,
But over the hills, where the seven dwarfs dwell,
Snow-White is still alive and well,
And none is so fair as she."

When she heard that, all her blood rushed to her heart with fear, for she saw plainly that little Snow-White was again alive. "But now," she said, "I will think of something that shall put an end to you," and by the help of witchcraft, which she understood, she made a poisonous comb. Then she disguised herself and took the shape of another old woman. So she went over the seven mountains to the seven dwarfs, knocked at the door, and cried: "Good things to sell, cheap, cheap!" Little Snow-White looked out and said: "Go away; I cannot let any one come in." "I suppose you can look," said the old woman, and pulled the poisonous comb out and held it up. It pleased the girl so well that she let herself be beguiled, and opened the door. When they had made a bargain the old woman said: "Now I will comb you properly for once." Poor little Snow-White had no suspicion, and let the old woman do as she pleased, but hardly had she put the comb in her hair than the poison in it took effect, and the girl fell down senseless. "You paragon of beauty," said the wicked woman, "you are done for now," and she went away.
But fortunately it was almost evening, when the seven dwarfs came home. When they saw Snow-White lying as if dead upon the ground they at once suspected the step-mother, and they looked and found the poisoned comb. Scarcely had they taken it out when Snow-White came to herself, and told them what had happened. Then they warned her once more to be upon her guard and to open the door to no one. The Queen, at home, went in front of the glass and said:

"Looking-glass, looking-glass, on the wall, who in this land is the fairest of all?"

then it answered as before: "Oh, Queen, thou art fairest of all I see,
But over the hills, where the seven dwarfs dwell,
Snow-White is still alive and well,
And none is so fair as she."

171

When she heard the glass speak thus she trembled and shook with rage. "Snow-White shall die," she cried, "even if it costs me my life!"

Thereupon she went into a quite secret, lonely room, where no one ever came, and there she made a very poisonous apple. Outside it looked pretty, white with a red cheek, so that everyone who saw it longed for it; but whoever ate a piece of it must surely die. When the apple was ready she painted her face, and dressed herself up as a country-woman, and so she went over the seven mountains to the seven dwarfs. She knocked at the door. Snow-White put her head out of the window and said: "I cannot let any one in; the seven dwarfs have forbidden me." "It is all the same to me," answered the woman, "I shall soon get rid of my apples. There, I will give you one."

"No," said Snow-White, "I dare not take anything." — "Are you afraid of poison?" said the old woman; "look, I will cut the apple in two pieces; you eat the red cheek, and I will eat the white." The apple was so cunningly made that only the red cheek was poisoned. Snow-White longed for the fine apple, and when she saw that the woman ate part of it she could resist no longer, and stretched out her hand and took the poisonous half. But hardly had she a bit of it in her mouth than she fell down dead. Then the Queen looked at her with a dreadful look, and laughed aloud and said: "White as snow, red as blood, black as ebony-wood! this time the dwarfs cannot wake you up again." And when she asked of the looking-glass at home:

"Looking-glass, looking-glass, on the wall, who in this land is the fairest of all?"

it answered at last: "Oh, Queen, in this land thou art fairest of all."

Then her envious heart had rest, so far as an envious heart can have rest. The dwarfs, when they came home in the evening, found Snow-White lying upon the ground; she breathed no longer and was dead. They lifted her up, looked to see whether they could find anything poisonous, unlaced her, combed her hair, washed her with water and wine, but it was all of no use; the poor child was dead, and remained dead. They laid her upon a bier, and all seven of them sat round it and wept for her, and wept three days long.

172

Then they were going to bury her, but she still looked as if she were living, and still had her pretty red cheeks. They said: "We could not bury her in the dark ground," and they had a transparent coffin of glass made, so that she could be seen from all sides, and they laid her in it, and wrote her name upon it in golden letters, and that she was a king's daughter. Then they put the coffin out upon the mountain, and one of them always stayed by it and watched it. And birds came too, and wept for Snow-White; first an owl, then a raven, and last a dove.

And now Snow-White lay a long, long time in the coffin, and she did not change, but looked as if she were asleep; for she was as white as snow, as red as blood, and her hair was as black as ebony.

It happened, however, that a king's son came into the forest, and went to the dwarfs' house to spend the night. He saw the coffin on the mountain, and the beautiful Snow-White within it, and read what was written upon it in golden letters. Then he said to the dwarfs: "Let me have the coffin, I will give you whatever you want for it." But the dwarfs answered: "We will not part with it for all the gold in the world." Then he said: "Let me have it as a gift, for I cannot live without

174

seeing Snow-White. I will honour and prize her as my dearest possession." As he spoke in this way the good dwarfs took pity upon him, and gave him the coffin. And now the King's son had it carried away by his servants on their shoulders. And it happened that they stumbled over a tree-stump, and with the shock the poisonous piece of apple which Snow-White had bitten off came out of her throat. And before long she opened her eyes, lifted up the lid of the coffin, sat up, and was once more alive. "Oh, heavens, where am I?" she cried. The King's son, full of joy, said: "You are with me," and told her what had happened, and said, "I love you more than everything in the world; come with me to my father's palace, you shall be my wife." And Snow-White was willing, and went with him, and their wedding was held with great show and splendour. But Snow-White's wicked step-mother was also bidden to the feast. When she had arrayed herself in beautiful clothes she went before the looking-glass, and said:

"Looking-glass, looking-glass, on the wall, who in this land is the fairest of all?"

the glass answered: "Oh, Queen, of all here the fairest art thou,
But the young Queen is fairer by far as I trow."

Then the wicked woman uttered a curse, and was so wretched, so utterly wretched, that she knew not what to do. At first she would not go to the wedding at all, but she had no peace, and must go to see the young Queen. And when she went in she knew Snow-White; and she stood still with rage and fear, and could not stir. But iron slippers had already been put upon the fire, and they were brought in with tongs, and set before her. Then she was forced to put on the red-hot shoes, and dance until she dropped down dead.

175

176

Cinderella

Illustrated by Birgit Amadori

The wife of a rich man fell sick, and as she felt that her end was drawing near, she called her only daughter to her bedside and said: "Dear child, be good and pious, and then the good God will always protect thee, and I will look down on thee from heaven and be near thee." Thereupon she closed her eyes and departed. Every day the maiden went out to her mother's grave, and wept, and she remained pious and good. When winter came the snow spread a white sheet over the grave, and when the spring sun had drawn it off again, the man had taken another wife.

The woman had brought two daughters into the house with her, who were beautiful and fair of face, but vile and black of heart. Now began a bad time for the poor step-child. "Is the stupid goose to sit in the parlour with us?" said they. "He who wants to eat bread must earn it; out with the kitchen-wench." They took her pretty clothes away from her, put an old grey bedgown on her, and gave her wooden shoes. "Just look at the proud princess, how decked out she is!" they cried, and laughed, and led her into the kitchen. There she had to do hard work from morning till night, get up before daybreak, carry water, light fires, cook and wash. Besides this, the sisters did her every imaginable injury – they mocked her and emptied her peas and lentils into the ashes, so that she was forced to sit and pick them out again. In the evening when she had worked till she was weary she had no bed to go to, but had to sleep by the fireside in the ashes. And as on that account she always looked dusty and dirty, they called her Cinderella. It happened that the father was once going to the fair, and he asked his two step-daughters what he should bring back for them. "Beautiful dresses," said one. "Pearls and jewels," said the second. "And thou, Cinderella," said he, "what wilt thou have?"

"Father, break off for me the first branch which knocks against your hat on your way home." So he bought beautiful dresses, pearls and jewels for his two step-daughters, and on his way home, as he was riding through a green thicket, a hazel twig brushed against him and knocked off his hat. Then he broke off the branch and took it with him. When he reached home he gave his step-daughters the things which they had wished for, and to Cinderella he gave the branch from the hazel-bush. Cinderella thanked him, went to her mother's grave and planted the branch on it, and wept so much that the tears fell down on it and watered it. And it grew, however, and became a handsome tree. Thrice a day Cinderella went and sat beneath it, and wept and prayed, and a little white bird always came on the tree, and if Cinderella expressed a wish, the bird threw down to her what she had wished for.

It happened, however, that the King appointed a festival which was to last three days, and to which all the beautiful young girls in the country were invited, in order that his son might choose himself a bride. When the two step-sisters heard that they too were to appear among the number, they were delighted, called

Cinderella and said: "Comb our hair for us, brush our shoes and fasten our buckles, for we are going to the festival at the King's palace." Cinderella obeyed, but wept, because she too would have liked to go with them to the dance, and begged her step-mother to allow her to do so. "Thou go, Cinderella!" said she; "Thou art dusty and dirty and wouldst go to the festival? Thou hast no clothes and shoes, and yet wouldst dance!" As, however, Cinderella went on asking, the step-mother at last said: "I have emptied a dish of lentils into the ashes for thee, if thou hast picked them out again in two hours, thou shalt go with us." The maiden went through the back-door into the garden, and called: "You tame pigeons, you turtle-doves, and all you birds beneath the sky, come and help me to pick:

The good into the pot, the bad into the crop."

Then two white pigeons came in by the kitchen-window, and afterwards the turtle-doves, and at last all the birds beneath the sky, came whirring and crowding in, and alighted amongst the ashes. And the pigeons nodded with their heads and began pick, pick, pick, pick, and the rest began also pick, pick, pick, pick, and gathered all the good grains into the dish. Hardly had one hour passed before they had finished, and all flew out again. Then the girl took the dish to her step-mother, and was glad, and believed that now she would be allowed to go with them to the festival. But the step-mother said: "No, Cinderella, thou hast no clothes and thou canst not dance; thou wouldst only be laughed at." And as Cinderella wept at this, the step-mother said: "If thou canst pick two dishes of lentils out of the ashes for me in one hour, thou shalt go with us." And she thought to herself: "That she most certainly cannot do." When the step-mother had emptied the two dishes of lentils amongst the ashes, the maiden went through the back-door into the garden and cried: "You tame pigeons, you turtle-doves, and all you birds under heaven, come and help me to pick:

The good into the pot, the bad into the crop."

Then two white pigeons came in by the kitchen-window, and afterwards the turtle-doves, and at length all the birds beneath the sky, came whirring and crowding in, and alighted amongst the ashes. And the doves nodded with their heads and began pick, pick, pick, pick, and the others began also pick, pick, pick, pick, and gathered all the good seeds into the dishes, and before half an hour was over they had already finished, and all flew out again. Then the maiden carried the dishes to the step-mother and was delighted, and believed that she might now go with them to the festival. But the step-mother said: "All this will not help thee; thou goest not with us, for thou hast no clothes and canst not dance; we should be ashamed of thee!" On this she turned her back on Cinderella, and hurried away with her two proud daughters. As no one was now at home, Cinderella went to her mother's grave beneath the hazel-tree, and cried,

"Shiver and quiver, little tree, silver and gold throw down over me."

Then the bird threw a gold and silver dress down to her, and slippers embroidered with silk and silver. She put on the dress with all speed, and went to the festival. Her step-sisters and the step-mother however did not know her, and thought she

must be a foreign princess, for she looked so beautiful in the golden dress. They never once thought of Cinderella, and believed that she was sitting at home in the dirt, picking lentils out of the ashes. The prince went to meet her, took her by the hand and danced with her. He would dance with no other maiden, and never left loose of her hand, and if any one else came to invite her, he said: "This is my partner."

She danced till it was evening, and then she wanted to go home. But the King's son said: "I will go with thee and bear thee company," for he wished to see to whom the beautiful maiden belonged. She escaped from him, however, and sprang into the pigeon-house. The King's son waited until her father came, and then he told him that the stranger maiden had leapt into the pigeon-house. The old man thought: "Can it be Cinderella?" and they had to bring him an axe and a pickaxe that he might hew the pigeon-house to pieces, but no one was inside it. And when they got home Cinderella lay in her dirty clothes among the ashes, and a dim little oil-lamp was burning on the mantle-piece, for Cinderella had jumped quickly down from the back of the pigeon-house and had run to the little hazel-tree, and there she had taken off her beautiful clothes and laid them on the grave, and the bird had taken them away again, and then she had placed herself in the kitchen amongst the ashes in her grey gown.

Next day when the festival began afresh, and her parents and the step-sisters had gone once more, Cinderella went to the hazel-tree and said:

"Shiver and quiver, my little tree, silver and gold throw down over me."

Then the bird threw down a much more beautiful dress than on the preceding day. And when Cinderella appeared at the festival in this dress, every one was astonished at her beauty. The King's son had waited until she came, and instantly took her by the hand and danced with no one but her. When others came and invited her, he said: "She is my partner."

When evening came she wished to leave, and the King's son followed her and wanted to see into which house she went. But she sprang away from him, and into the garden behind the house. Therein stood a beautiful tall tree on which hung the

184

most magnificent pears. She clambered so nimbly between the branches like a squirrel that the King's son did not know where she was gone. He waited until her father came, and said to him: "The stranger-maiden has escaped from me, and I believe she has climbed up the pear-tree." The father thought: "Can it be Cinderella?" and had an axe brought and cut the tree down, but no one was on it. And when they got into the kitchen, Cinderella lay there amongst the ashes, as usual, for she had jumped down on the other side of the tree, had taken the beautiful dress to the bird on the little hazel-tree, and put on her grey gown.

On the third day, when the parents and sisters had gone away, Cinderella went once more to her mother's grave and said to the little tree:

"Shiver and quiver, my little tree, silver and gold throw down over me."

And now the bird threw down to her a dress which was more splendid and magnificent than any she had yet had, and the slippers were golden. And when she went to the festival in the dress, no one knew how to speak for astonishment. The King's son danced with her only, and if any one invited her to dance, he said: "She is my partner."

When evening came, Cinderella wished to leave, and the King's son was anxious to go with her, but she escaped from him so quickly that he could not follow her. The King's son had, however, used a strategem, and had caused the whole staircase to be smeared with pitch, and there, when she ran down, had the maiden's left slipper remained sticking. The King's son picked it up, and it was small and dainty, and all golden. Next morning, he went with it to the father, and said to him: "No one shall be my wife but she whose foot this golden slipper fits." Then were the two sisters glad, for they had pretty feet. The eldest went with the shoe into her room and wanted to try it on, and her mother stood by. But she could not get her big toe into it, and the shoe was too small for her. Then her mother gave her a knife and said: "Cut the toe off; when thou art Queen thou wilt have no more need to go on foot." The maiden cut the toe off, forced the foot into the shoe, swallowed the pain, and went out to the King's son. Then he took her on his horse as his bride and rode away with her. They were, however, obliged to pass the grave, and there, on the hazel-tree, sat the two pigeons and cried:

"Turn and peep, turn and peep,
There's blood within the shoe,
The shoe it is too small for her,
The true bride waits for you."

Then he looked at her foot and saw how the blood was streaming from it. He turned his horse round and took the false bride home again, and said she was not the true one, and that the other sister was to put the shoe on. Then this one went into her chamber and got her toes safely into the shoe, but her heel was too large. So her mother gave her a knife and said: "Cut a bit off thy heel; when thou art Queen thou wilt have no more need to go on foot." The maiden cut a bit off her heel, forced her foot into the shoe, swallowed the pain, and went out to the King's son. He took her on his horse as his bride, and rode away with her, but when they passed by the hazel-tree, two little pigeons sat on it and cried,

"Turn and peep, turn and peep,
There's blood within the shoe
The shoe it is too small for her,
The true bride waits for you."

He looked down at her foot and saw how the blood was running out of her shoe, and how it had stained her white stocking. Then he turned his horse and took the false bride home again. "This also is not the right one," said he, "have you no other daughter?" — "No," said the man, "There is still a little stunted kitchen-wench which my late wife left behind her, but she cannot possibly be the bride." The King's son said he was to send her up to him; but the mother answered: "Oh, no, she is much too dirty, she cannot show herself!" He absolutely insisted on it, and Cinderella had to be called. She first washed her hands and face clean, and then went and bowed down before the King's son, who gave her the golden shoe. Then she seated herself on a stool, drew her foot out of the heavy wooden shoe, and put it into the slipper, which fitted like a glove. And when she rose up and the King's son looked at her face he recognized the beautiful maiden who had danced with him and cried: "That is the true bride!" The step-mother and the two sisters were terrified and became pale with rage; he, however, took Cinderella on his horse and rode away with her. As they passed by the hazel-tree, the two white doves cried:

"Turn and peep, turn and peep,
No blood is in the shoe,
The shoe is not too small for her,
The true bride rides with you,"

and when they had cried that, the two came flying down and placed themselves on Cinderella's shoulders, one on the right, the other on the left, and remained sitting there.

When the wedding with the King's son had to be celebrated, the two false sisters came and wanted to get into favour with Cinderella and share her good fortune. When the betrothed couple went to church, the elder was at the right side and the younger at the left, and the pigeons pecked out one eye of each of them. Afterwards as they came back, the elder was at the left, and the younger at the right, and then the pigeons pecked out the other eye of each. And thus, for their wickedness and falsehood, they were punished with blindness as long as they lived.

Godfather Death

Illustrated by Jan Ø. Callesen

A poor man had twelve children and was forced to work night and day to give them even bread. When therefore the thirteenth came into the world, he knew not what to do in his trouble, but ran out into the great highway, and resolved to ask the first person whom he met to be godfather. The first to meet him was the good God who already knew what filled his heart, and said to him: "Poor man, I pity thee. I will hold thy child at its christening, and will take charge of it and make it happy on earth." The man said: "Who art thou?" — "I am God." — "Then I do not desire to have thee for a godfather," said the man; "thou givest to the rich, and leavest the poor to hunger." Thus spoke the man, for he did not know how wisely God apportions riches and poverty. He turned therefore away from the Lord, and went farther. Then the Devil came to him and said: "What seekest thou? If thou wilt take me as a godfather for thy child, I will give him gold in plenty and all the joys of the world as well." The man asked: "Who art thou?" — "I am the Devil." "Then I do not desire to have thee for godfather," said the man; "thou deceivest men and leadest them astray." He went onwards, and then came Death striding up to him with withered legs, and said: "Take me as godfather." The man asked: "Who art thou?" — "I am Death, and I make all equal." Then said the man: "Thou art the right one, thou takest the rich as well as the poor, without distinction; thou shalt be godfather." Death answered: "I will make thy child rich and famous, for he who has me for a friend can lack nothing." The man said: "Next Sunday is the christening; be there at the right time." Death appeared as he had promised, and stood godfather quite in the usual way.

When the boy had grown up, his godfather one day appeared and bade him go with him. He led him forth into a forest, and showed him a herb which grew there, and said: "Now shalt thou receive thy godfather's present. I make thee a celebrated physician. When thou art called to a patient, I will always appear to thee. If I stand by the head of the sick man, thou mayst say with confidence that thou wilt make him well again, and if thou givest him of this herb he will recover; but if I stand by the patient's feet, he is mine, and thou must say that all remedies are in vain, and that no physician in the world could save him. But beware of using the herb against my will, or it might fare ill with thee."

It was not long before the youth was the most famous physician in the whole world. "He had only to look at the patient and he knew his condition at once, and if he would recover, or must needs die." So they said of him, and from far and wide people came to him, sent for him when they had any one ill, and gave him so much money that he soon became a rich man. Now it so befell that the King became ill, and the physician was summoned, and was to say if recovery were possible. But when he came to the bed, Death was standing by the feet of the sick man, and the herb did not grow which could save him. "If I could but cheat Death for once," thought the physician, "he is sure to take it ill if I do, but, as I am his godson, he will shut one eye; I will risk it." He therefore took up the sick man, and laid him the other way, so that now Death was standing by his head. Then he gave the King some of the herb, and he recovered and grew healthy again. But Death came to the physician, looking very black and angry, threatened him with his finger, and said: "Thou hast overreached me; this time I will pardon it, as thou art my godson; but if thou venturest it again, it will cost thee thy neck, for I will take thee thyself away with me."

Soon afterwards the King's daughter fell into a severe illness. She was his only child, and he wept day and night, so that he began to lose the sight of his eyes, and he caused it to be made known that whosoever rescued her from death should be her husband and inherit the crown. When the physician came to the sick girl's bed, he saw Death by her feet. He ought to have remembered the warning given by his godfather, but he was so infatuated by the great beauty of the King's daughter, and the happiness of becoming her husband, that he flung all thought to the winds. He did not see that Death was casting angry glances on him, that he was raising his hand in the air, and threatening him with his withered fist. He

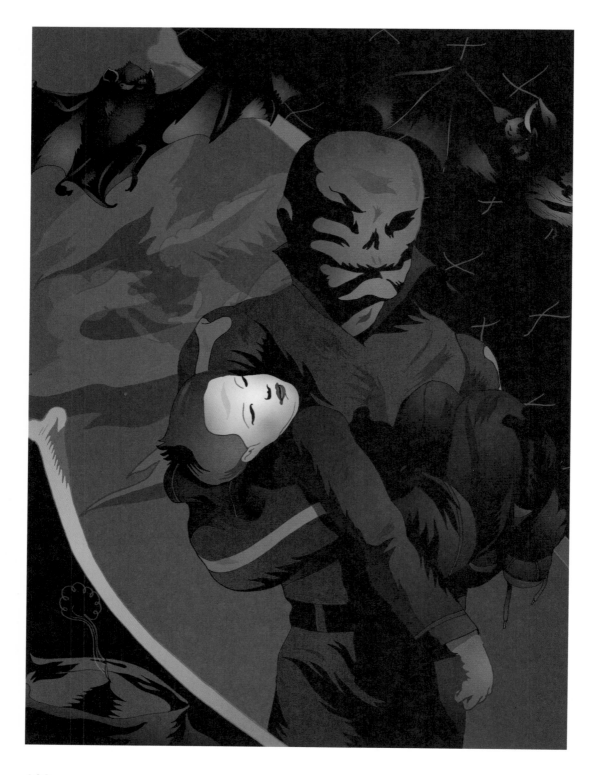

raised up the sick girl, and placed her head where her feet had lain. Then he gave her some of the herb, and instantly her cheeks flushed red, and life stirred afresh in her.

When Death saw that for a second time he was defrauded of his own property, he walked up to the physician with long strides, and said: "All is over with thee, and now the lot falls on thee," and seized him so firmly with his ice-cold hand, that he could not resist, and led him into a cave below the earth. There he saw how thousands and thousands of candles were burning in countless rows, some large, others half-sized, others small. Every instant some were extinguished, and others again burnt up, so that the flames seemed to leap hither and thither in perpetual change. "See," said Death, "these are the lights of men's lives. The large ones belong to children, the half-sized ones to married people in their prime, the little ones belong to old people; but children and young folks likewise have often only a tiny candle." — "Show me the light of my life," said the physician, and he thought that it would be still very tall. Death pointed to a little end which was just threatening to go out, and said: "Behold, it is there." — "Ah, dear godfather," said the horrified physician, "light a new one for me, do it for love of me, that I may enjoy my life, be King, and the husband of the King's beautiful daughter." — "I cannot," answered Death, "one must go out before a new one is lighted." — "Then place the old one on a new one, that will go on burning at once when the old one has come to an end," pleaded the physician. Death behaved as if he were going to fulfill his wish, and took hold of a tall new candle; but as he desired to revenge himself, he purposely made a mistake in fixing it, and the little piece fell down and was extinguished. Immediately the physician fell on the ground, and now he himself was in the hands of Death.

194

The Golden Goose

Illustrated by Nathalie Nystad

There was a man who had three sons, the youngest of whom was called Dummling, and was despised, mocked, and sneered at on every occasion. It happened that the eldest wanted to go into the forest to hew wood, and before he went his mother gave him a beautiful sweet cake and a bottle of wine in order that he might not suffer from hunger or thirst. When he entered the forest he met a little grey-haired old man who bade him good-day, and said: "Do give me a piece of cake out of your pocket, and let me have a draught of your wine, I am so hungry and thirsty." But the clever son answered: "If I give you my cake and wine, I shall have none for myself, be off with you," and he left the little man standing and went on. But when he began to hew down a tree, it was not long before he made a false stroke, and the axe cut him in the arm, so that he had to go home and have it bound up. And this was the little grey man's doing. After this the second son went into the forest, and his mother gave him, like the eldest, a cake and a bottle of wine. The little old grey man met him likewise, and asked him for a piece of cake and a drink of wine. But the second son, too, said sensibly enough: "What I give you will be taken away from myself, be off," and he left the little man standing and went on. His punishment, however, was not delayed, when he had made a few blows at the tree he struck himself in the leg, so that he had to be carried home. Then Dummling said: "Father, do let me go and cut wood." The father answered: "Your brothers have hurt themselves with it, leave it alone, you do not understand anything about it." But Dummling begged so long that at last he said: "Just go then, you will get wiser by hurting yourself." His mother gave him a cake made with water and baked in the cinders, and with it a bottle of sour beer. When he came to the forest the little old grey man met him likewise, and greeting him, said: "Give me a piece of your cake and a drink out of your bottle, I am so hungry and thirsty." Dummling answered: "I have only cinder-cake and sour beer, if that pleases you, we will sit down and eat." So they sat down, and when Dummling pulled out his cinder-cake, it was a fine sweet cake, and the sour beer had become good wine. So they ate and drank, and after that the little man said: "Since you have a good heart, and are willing to divide what you have, I will give you good luck. There stands an old tree, cut it down, and you will find something at the roots." Then the little man took leave of him. Dummling went and cut down the tree, and when it fell there was a goose sitting in the roots with feathers of pure gold. He lifted her up, and taking her with him, went to an inn where he thought he would stay the night. Now the host had three daughters, who saw the goose and were curious to know what such a wonderful bird might be, and would have liked to have one of its golden feathers. The eldest thought, I shall soon find an opportunity of pulling out a feather, and as soon as Dummling had gone out she seized the goose by the wing, but her finger and hand remained sticking fast to it. The second came soon afterwards, thinking only of how she might get a feather

196

for herself, but she had scarcely touched her sister than she was held fast. At last the third also came with the like intent, and the others screamed out: "Keep away, for goodness, sake keep away." But she did not understand why she was to keep away. The others are there, she thought, I may as well be there too, and ran to them, but as soon as she had touched her sister, she remained sticking fast to her. So they had to spend the night with the goose. The next morning Dummling took the goose under his arm and set out, without troubling himself about the three girls who were hanging onto it. They were obliged to run after him continually, now left, now right, wherever his legs took him. In the middle of the fields the parson met them, and when he saw the procession he said: "For shame, you good-for-nothing girls, why are you running across the fields after this young man. Is that seemly?" At the same time he seized the youngest by the hand in order to pull her away, but as soon as he touched her he likewise stuck fast, and was himself obliged to run behind. Before long the sexton came by and saw his master, the parson, running behind three girls. He was astonished at this and called out: "Hi, your reverence, whither away so quickly. Do not forget that we have a christening today," and running after him he took him by the sleeve, but was also held fast to it. Whilst the five were trotting thus one behind the other, two laborers came with their hoes from the fields, the parson called out to them and begged that they would set him and the sexton free. But they had scarcely touched the sexton when they were held fast, and now there were seven of them running behind Dummling and the goose. Soon afterwards he came to a city, where a king ruled who had a daughter who was so serious that no one could make her laugh. So he had put forth a decree that whosoever should be able to make her laugh should marry her. When Dummling heard this, he went with his goose and all her train before the king's daughter, and as soon as she saw the seven people running on and on, one behind the other, she began to laugh quite loudly, and as if she would never stop. Thereupon Dummling asked to have her for his wife, but the king did not like the son-in-law, and made all manner of excuses and said he must first produce a man who could drink a cellarful of wine. Dummling thought of the little grey man, who could certainly help him, so he went into the forest, and in the same place where he had felled the tree, he saw a man sitting, who had a very sorrowful face. Dummling asked him what he was taking to heart so sorely, and he answered: "I have such a great thirst and cannot quench it, cold water I cannot stand, a barrel of wine I have just emptied, but that to me is like a drop on a hot stone." - "There, I can help you," said Dummling, "just come with me and you shall be satisfied." He led him into the king's cellar, and the man bent over the huge barrels, and drank and drank till his loins hurt, and before the day was out he had emptied all the barrels. Then Dummling asked once more for his bride, but the king was vexed that such an ugly fellow, whom everyone called Dummling, should take away his daughter, and he made a new condition, he must first find a man who could eat a whole mountain of bread. Dummling did not think long, but went straight into the forest, where in the same place there sat a man wastying up his body with a strap, and making an awful face, and saying: "I have eaten a whole ovenful of rolls, but what good is that when one has such a hunger as I. My stomach remains empty, and I must tie myself up if I am not to die of hunger." At this Dummling was glad, and said: "Get up and come with me, you shall eat yourself full." He led him to the king's palace,

200

where all the flour in the whole kingdom was collected, and from it he caused a huge mountain of bread to be baked. The man from the forest stood before it, began to eat, and by the end of one day the whole mountain had vanished. Then Dummling for the third time asked for his bride, but the king again sought a way out, and ordered a ship which could sail on land and on water. "As soon as you come sailing back in it," said he, "you shall have my daughter for wife." Dummling went straight into the forest, and there sat the little grey man to whom he had given his cake. When he heard what Dummling wanted, he said: "Since you have given me to eat and to drink, I will give you the ship, and I do all this because you once were kind to me." Then he gave him the ship which could sail on land and water, and when the king saw that, he could no longer prevent him from having his daughter. The wedding was celebrated, and after the king's death, Dummling inherited his kingdom and lived for a longtime contentedly with his wife.

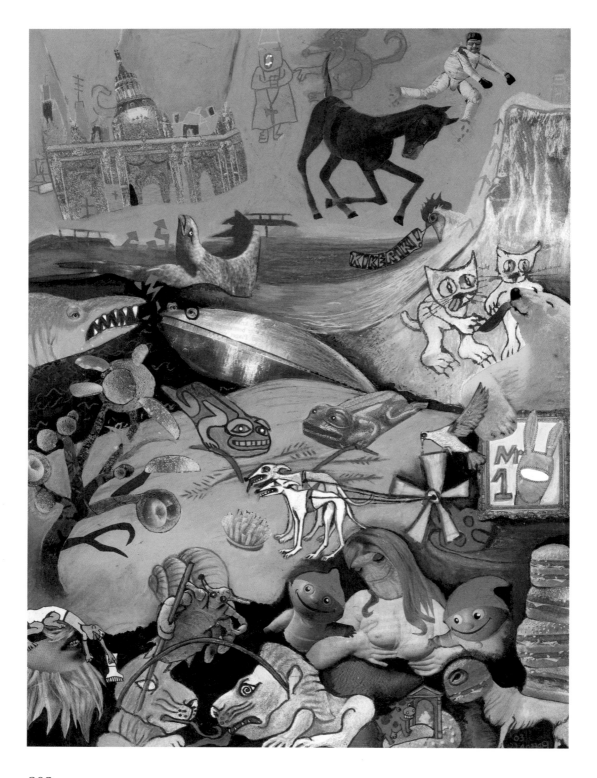

202

The Story of Schlauraffenland

Illustrated by Dead Chickens

In the time of Schlauraffen I went there, and saw Rome and the Lateran hanging by a small silken thread, and a man without feet who outran a swift horse, and a keen sharp sword that cut through a bridge. There I saw a young ass with a silver nose which pursued two fleet hares, and a lime-tree that was very large, on which hot cakes were growing. There I saw a lean old goat which carried about a hundred cart-loads of fat on his body, and sixty loads of salt. Have I not told enough lies? There I saw a plough ploughing without horse or cow, and a child of one year threw four millstones from Ratisbon to Treves, and from Treves to Strasburg, and a hawk swam over the Rhine, which he had a perfect right to do. There I heard some fishes begin to make such a disturbance with each other, that it resounded as far as heaven, and sweet honey flowed like water from a deep valley at the top of a high mountain, and these were strange things. There were two crows which were mowing a meadow, and I saw two gnats building a bridge, and two doves tore a wolf to pieces; two children brought forth two kids, and two frogs threshed corn together. There I saw two mice consecrating a bishop, and two cats scratching out a bear's tongue. Then a snail came running up and killed two furious lions. There stood a barber and shaved a woman's beard off; and two sucking-children bade their mother hold her tongue. There I saw two greyhounds which brought a mill out of the water; and a sorry old horse was beside it, and said it was right. And four horses were standing in the yard threshing corn with all their might, and two goats were heating the stove, and a red cow shot the bread into the oven. Then a cock crowed, Cock-a-doodle-doo! The story is all told,

Cock-a-doodle-doo!

The Illustrators:

A-Linha a.k.a. Clarissa Tossin
"Mother Holle"
Lives and works in São Paulo, Brazil.
mail: clarissa@a-linha.org / url: www.a-linha.org

Annlaug Auestad
"The Valiant Little Tailor"
Lives and works in Stavanger, Norway.
mail: annlaug@stavanger-illustratorene.no / url: www.stavanger-illustratorene.no

Birgit Amadori
"Cinderella"
Lives and works in Darmstadt, Germany.
mail: birgit.amadori@t-online.de / url: www.amadori.org

Christian Montenegro
"King Thrushbeard"
Lives and works in Buenos Aires, Argentina.
mail: montenegrochristian@hotmail.com/ url: www.christianmontenegro.com.ar

Dan Abbott
"The Wishing-Table, Gold-Ass, and the Cudgel in the Sack"
Lives and works in London, UK.
mail: mister.dan@virgin.net

Dead Chickens

"The Story of Schlauraffenland"
Live and work in Berlin, Germany.
mail: breeda.c.c.@deadchickens.de / url: www.dead-chickens.de

Deanne Cheuk

"The Star-Money"
Lives and works in New York, USA.
mail: neomuworld@aol.com / url: www.neomu.com

Emma Åkerman

"Rumpelstiltskin"
Lives and studies in Stockholm, Sweden.
mail: emma.akerman@konstfack.se

Erotic Dragon a.k.a. Miho Tei

"Briar-Rose"
Lives and works in Tokyo, Japan.
mail: miho@eroticdragon.com / url: www.eroticdragon.com

Hendrik Hellige

"Story of the Youth Who Went Forth to Learn What Fear Was"
Lives and works in Berlin, Germany.
mail: henni@die-gestalten.de

Jan Ø. Callesen

"Godfather Death"
Lives and works in Copenhagen, Denmark.
mail: jan@gulstue.com / url: www.jancallesen.dk

Judith Drews & Hans Baltzer
"The Wolf and the Seven Little Kids"
Judith lives and studies in Hamburg, Hans lives and works in Berlin, Germany.
mail: post@judithdrews.de, hans@garage-g.de / url: www.judithdrews.de

Judith Zaugg
"Hansel & Grethel"
Lives and works in Bern, Switzerland.
mail: contact@judithzaugg.ch / url: www.judithzaugg.ch

Katrin Petursdottir
"Jorinda & Joringel"
Lives and works in Reykjavik, Iceland.
mail: katrin@simnet.is

Kinpro a.k.a. Shinya Chisato
"Little Snow-White"
Lives and works in Tokyo, Japan.
mail: kinpro8@yahoo.co.jp / url: www.iacnet.ne.jp/~kinpro

Koraters a.k.a. Shoko Nakazawa
"Hans in Luck"
Lives and works in Tokyo, Japan.
mail: shoko@koraters.com / url: www.koraters.com

Koshiro Torisu
"The Bremen Town-Musicians"
Lives and works in Paris, France.
mail: hello@torisukoshiro.com / url: www.torisukoshiro.com

Kyotarow Aoki
"Thumbling"
Lives and works in Tokyo, Japan.
mail: kyotarow@sweet.ocn.ne.jp / url: www11.ocn.ne.jp/~kyotarow

Margit Fellerer
"Snow-White & Rose-Red"
Lives and works in Berlin, Germany.
mail: mf@pury.org / url: www.pury.org

Michał Książek
"The Frog-King"
Lives and works in Wrocław, Poland.
mail: xmicha@wp.pl / url: www.ksiazek.prv.pl

Nathalie Nystad
"The Golden Goose"
Lives and works in Copenhagen, Denmark.
mail: info@popkorn.org / url: www.popkorn.org

Pia Wall
"Rapunzel"
Lives and works in Stavanger, Norway.
mail: pia@stavanger-illustratorene.no / url: www.stavanger-illustratorene.no

Rilla Alexander
"Little Red-Cap"
Lives and works in Brisbane, Australia.
mail: rilla@rinzen.com / url: www.sozi.com, www.rinzen.com

Grimm – The Illustrated Fairy Tales of the Brothers Grimm
by Jacob & Wilhelm Grimm

Edited by Robert Klanten and Hendrik Hellige
Layout/Project Management: Hendrik Hellige
Proofreading: Helga Beck and Michael Robinson
Production Management: Janni Milstrey
Production Assistant: Vinzenz Geppert
Cover Illustration: Erotic Dragon

Made in Singapore.

Bibliographic information published by Die Deutsche Bibliothek.
Die Deutsche Bibliothek lists this publication in the Deutsche Nationalbibliografie;
detailed bibliographic data is available in the Internet at http://dnb.ddb.de.

ISBN 3-89955-028-5

For more information please check www.die-gestalten.de.

Respect copyright, encourage creativity!